THE
COUNTRY
DOCTOR'S
DAUGHTER

BY
GILL SANDERSON

MILLS & BOON®
Pure reading pleasure™

First published in Great Britain 2009
Harlequin Mills & Boon Limited,
Eton House, 18-24 Paradise Road, Richmond, Surrey TW9 1SR

© Gill Sanderson 2009

ISBN: 978 0 263 86855 5

Set in Times Roman 10½ on 12¾ pt
03-0709-49928

Printed and bound in Spain
by Litografia Rosés, S.A., Barcelona

THE
COUNTRY
DOCTOR'S
DAUGHTER

For Sweetpea—Wuv you.

CHAPTER ONE

DR KELLY BLACKMAN liked walking in the sunshine. Here, the sun wasn't too hot or the air too dry and the wind didn't blow sand so that… Here, on the south coast of Brittany things were just fine.

Well, as fine as they could be. Finer than they had been over the past six months. For a start, all that was left of the injury to her leg was a scar that was easily disguised. Not that that had ever been so important.

She had been ill, really ill. But now it was over, she was cured. She was starting a new life. And if at first she felt a little uncertain, not sure of where she was going or what she wanted, well, that was to be expected. She'd planned an easy start for a month or so—and then on to anywhere in the world!

She had thought this path would be deserted. But in the distance she saw a man coming towards her and she veered away from the cliff edge, headed through the gorse. She'd go back to her cottage now, she didn't feel like another chat. She'd start being a friendly member of the community when she began work, in a week's time.

In fact, she recognised the man. He was the village

postman. That morning he had congratulated her on her French, and had obviously wanted to talk longer. But he had bright golden hair. Nothing wrong with that, it wasn't his fault, it just brought back memories of another man.

And the memories of the golden-haired man were still with her now, even though her other problem had completely disappeared.

She had always been ready to face her problems—perhaps too ready. So now she had to face up to the fact that Gary was gone, he was out of her life. She had torn up all his letters—not that there had been too many of them. She had thrown away the gifts he had given her. She'd offered him back the engagement ring—he had taken it. She wondered if he would try to sell it, or even keep it for the next woman he fooled.

Don't look back, look forward! Gary was gone, he wasn't worth bothering about! All right, for a while perhaps her behaviour had been hard to take, she must have been difficult to live with. But there had always been an end in sight, he'd known she was curable. She knew that if the situation had been reversed, she would have stood by him, would have been patient, would have been loving. Not Gary. He didn't do being patient. And then there was that last ultimate betrayal. So now she had to get over him. Another hurdle.

Would she ever meet, ever love another man? She doubted it. She just couldn't imagine offering any other man the unquestioning devotion she had given to Gary. Always, she would be cautious, afraid. Not a good beginning for any relationship.

She was nearly home now. In front of her was a tiny path

through the gorse, she guessed it would lead to the back of her cottage. It would be quicker to climb the slight rise in front of her, to walk back along the main road that led to the village. She could hear the hum of the occasional passing car, slowing as it negotiated the first of the hairpin bends that led down past her cottage into the village square. But she would stay here, where it was more pleasant.

She thought she'd enjoy her three months' stay in the whitewashed cottage. She'd be happy here in the little French seaside village of Riom. The cottage belonged to Dr Joe Cameron, an old friend—usually he lived in it while he acted as part-time doctor at a local practice. Kelly was taking over both the cottage and the part-time job; this year Joe was going to New Zealand to see his son and family.

It would be good to get back into medicine again. She was ready for it now—even eager for it. Joe had said that she was completely cured but to take it easy for a while. Work herself back into things. This was a job that would enable her to stay tranquil.

That was weird, she thought she could hear the sound of children singing. Next, she was half-conscious of the sound of an engine. A car was speeding down the hill, far too fast to negotiate the bends that… She didn't have time to complete the thought.

She had not expected this! Not straight away! For a while her life was supposed to be calm, uneventful, without any undue excitement. But suddenly she was there again, in the middle of it, the sounds so familiar, so terrible. The car must have crashed. There was the bang of a bursting tyre, the shriek of tortured metal. A moment or two later the softer but even more frightening 'woof' of fuel catching fire. And then, just faintly, the smell of burning petrol. And screams. Kelly winced. She knew this scene, she was back there!

Her body reacted before her brain did. She turned, ran up the slope that overlooked the road. In an accident sometimes even the first few seconds were important.

Her expert eye assessed the situation at once. An old Citroën minibus, lying on its side, jammed against a stone wall. A sign on the side said that it belonged to the École Élémentaire de Merveille. There were flames coming from somewhere but so far there had been no explosion. Two young children stood nearby. A door was open in the upturned side of the vehicle and a man with blood streaming down the side of his face was helping a crying child to climb out. There were still screams coming from inside but Kelly's trained ear detected that so far they were more screams of fear than actual physical pain. That was good— but only trouble could come from panic. A van full of children—how many available, useful adults?

For Kelly this was like old times, she automatically knew what to do. Assess what you saw. These were children, which made things worse, but the situation seemed ultimately containable. This was a management problem before it was a medical one.

First, she could do with expert help. Joe had told her that the doctor she was to work for, a Dr Luc Laforge, lived only five minutes' drive from the village. Kelly was to start work for him in a week's time, she had intended to phone him after she had settled into her cottage. But this was an emergency, she needed him now. She took out her mobile phone, called the pre-set number. Fortunately, there was an instant answer.

'Dr Laforge? This is Dr Blackman, I am to be your new locum doctor. A minibus has crashed and overturned here on the hill that runs down from Merveille into Riom. Children are injured, perhaps not seriously, but I need help.'

'I'll be there in five minutes, Dr Blackman.' He rang off.

Kelly nodded her satisfaction. This was a man who understood emergencies.

She walked to the side of the minibus, summoned up her French and told the three children to go to the far side of the road, sit high on the bank and not move. Then she heaved herself up onto the side of the vehicle, looked at the bleeding man.

'I'm a doctor, let me take charge. Have you got a first-aid kit, a fire extinguisher?'

The man was obviously shocked. 'The tyre burst,' he said plaintively, 'I was driving round the bend and the tyre burst.'

'Never mind that now! Do you have a first-aid kit, a fire extinguisher?'

She had to repeat her question. Be patient, the man was shocked. 'Under the front seat. They're both there.'

Kelly peered down. There appeared to be five children lying tumbled among the seats. Another man was trying to pull a child from under a pile of baggage.

'You,' Kelly snapped. 'Leave that child alone, I'll come and see to her. Pass me the fire extinguisher from under the front seat and then climb up here.'

Startled, the man did as he was told. Kelly handed the fire extinguisher to the bleeding man by her side. 'This should be good enough to put out the flames,' she said. 'When you've done that, walk up the road with your red triangle and make sure any oncoming traffic stops. We don't want another accident. Oh, and hold this to your face.' She took the silk scarf from round her neck and handed it to him.

The man stared at her. 'Do it now!' Kelly shouted. The man responded at once.

Kelly realised she was forgetting something. She was slipping. 'What is your name, please?' she asked the man now standing by her.

'I am Armand Leblanc. I am a teacher and I—'

'My name's Kelly, Kelly Blackman, and I'm an English doctor. Who's that who is putting out the fire?'

'That is François Moliere. He was our driver and I—'

'Armand and Francois, good. We can cope with this.'

In a situation like this, names were important. Call them by name and people felt they were part of a team, not a cog in a machine. Names made people more efficient.

'You stay out here, Armand, and I'll drop down to examine the children before we move them. When I pass them up to you, see that they sit quietly together at the far side of the road. Has François managed to put out the fire?'

'He has. He's walking up the road as you told him.'

'Good.'

She dropped into the vehicle and found herself kneeling on the side of a seat. Around her, like scattered dolls, were five children, aged, she guessed, about seven. Three were crying, one, who appeared to be trapped, was moaning, one was suspiciously silent. 'Children!' she called. 'This is an adventure. I know you're upset but soon you'll all be well and you can carry on with your trip. I want you all to remain absolutely still until I have looked at you. Now, I heard you singing. What is your favourite song, the one you were singing as you came down the hill?'

'"Frère Jacques",' a voice offered.

'Sing "Frère Jacques" to me. Loudly!'

A moment's silence. Then one quavering voice started and then one or two more. It was a start, Kelly thought.

First, a lightning ABC check on each child. Airway, breathing, circulation. All well so far. She bent over, scrabbled under the front seat and found the first-aid kit. It wasn't equipped for large-scale accidents like this but there would be something of use.

Next, the unconscious child. As Kelly knelt over her, her eyes twitched open and she groaned. Kelly looked into the eyes, one pupil was much more dilated than the other. Concussion. This child would need hospital care. She had forgotten again! 'Armand! Has anyone informed the police, asked for an ambulance?'

'I called on my mobile phone. But they might be some time.'

'Well done.'

Kelly felt round the back of the child's head, there was a bad gash there and more blood than she had realised. There was a lump but she didn't think the skull was fractured. Still, the gash needed immediate attention. Kelly found an emergency dressing, put it on the cut and then wrapped bandages tightly round the head. It was an improvised job but it was the kind of thing she had had to do before. It wasn't ideal but it was the best she could do and it would slow the bleeding.

Then, as far as possible, an examination of the rest of the body. Scratches, bruises, she didn't think there was anything more seriously wrong. But the child could rest here a minute.

Unbelievably, the three children who had been singing had finished their song—and had started another. Kelly shook her head.

She turned to the child who had been moaning, and winced. She didn't like the way the child's head was lolling to one side. She shook out the contents of the first-aid box—no hard collar.

She took bandages and a dressing from the first-aid kit, tried to adjust the child's head so that she couldn't move it. Probably none of the vertebrae would be damaged. But if one was damaged then any sudden movement could result in permanent paralysis of the lower body. Kelly had seen it happen.

Another quick check of the child's body, the usual scratches, a deep cut on one arm. Kelly wrapped a temporary dressing round the arm, patted the child's cheek and murmured, 'Rest there a while. Try not to move, I'll be back with you soon.'

And onto the other three. They seemed to be largely unhurt apart from minor injuries, which were quickly dressed. The children would have to be checked over in hospital, of course, that was essential. This was first aid, she was trying to ensure that they didn't get any worse until they could have proper medical attention.

She was about to ask Armand to help her out with the three largely uninjured children when she heard voices. And a second later there was another face looking down at her from the opened door above.

She shouldn't have had time to notice—but she did. It was an attractive face. Quite sunburned—as most of them were around here. Not really conventionally good looking but there were laughter lines round startlingly blue eyes, and his lips were curved and looked as if they liked to laugh as well.

Then his gaze shifted to the children's bodies lying around her and she saw the horror on his face. Too late, she remembered that she had been told that Dr Laforge had a daughter of about this age—and she had recently been injured in a car crash. What must he be feeling now?

But the doctor was a professional, here to do his job. She could tell it was an effort for him but his face went blank and he said, 'Dr Blackman, I'm Dr Laforge. What have you got for me?' He spoke to her in English.

His tone was cool, the voice not very welcoming, and Kelly didn't like the phrasing of his question. She was as much a doctor as he was, this was something that they should do together. Odd, his English was impeccable.

'Pleased to meet you, Dr Laforge. Have you got a hard collar with you? I'm not happy about this little girl, she seems to have strained her neck.'

'I always carry a full medical kit in my car.'

She saw him turn his head, heard him say, 'Please, could you fetch the large black bag out of the boot of my car?' Then he turned back to her and said, 'Dr Blackman, as I recollect, you are not yet insured to practise medicine in France.'

'No, I am not. Would you have preferred me to sit quietly by the roadside, filling out a formal application for permission?'

He smiled briefly, and for a moment she saw a different, more pleasant man, the change in his face was so great. 'Dr Blackman, you have done in France what I trust I would have done in England. But now, may I suggest that I take over the work here and you see to those who we can take out? I suspect there is only room for one doctor to work.'

'Of course,' she said. It made sense. But first she had to make her report. What she had observed, what she had done, what she thought was necessary. Dr Laforge listened and obviously approved. 'Good,' he said briefly.

She climbed out and the doctor took her place. He suggested, 'Shall we take out these three little girls who appear to be relatively unharmed? You look after them and then I'll do what I can for the two more seriously injured children.'

'Seems a good plan.'

Armand returned with a large black bag, handed it down to the doctor. When Kelly saw him take out a hard collar, she decided that there was little more she could do to help.

She now had six little girls sitting together by the roadside. First of all a quick but more detailed examination of each. She had brought the first-aid kit with her as Dr Laforge now had his own, much larger bag. There were a couple of cuts to dress, grazes to spread ointment on, but nothing serious. She moved them further up the bank so they were in the sun, made them huddle together to keep warm. No hot drink unfortunately—but that would come later. There was still the danger of shock, she had to make them feel loved and comfortable and at ease.

Of all things, her accent was the thing that amused them. She got them to correct her pronunciation, to tell her words that she claimed not to know. And the little girls laughed and loved it. No danger of shock.

Things started to move out of her hands then. Two ambulances arrived, with SAMU, the French equivalent of paramedics. They took over. The girls were quickly checked again, then loaded into the ambulances, Armand and François going with them. Dr Laforge made a brief report on each one and the ambulances drew away. Shortly afterwards, mechanics arrived with a big tow truck and started to work on the minibus. Kelly watched. These people were good.

And then Dr Laforge came striding across to speak to her. She didn't know if it was the right or the wrong time.

Up to now she had been in emergency medical mode, thinking of little but the immediate situation and the most effective way of dealing with it. Emotions had been put to one side. It was a state she knew well, she even enjoyed it. And this had been a comparatively minor incident compared with what she had dealt with in the past. But there was always a downside, a reaction when the work was over. And she wondered if the downside would be worse today. It had been months since she had dealt with even a small emergency. She would really like to get home, to get to the peace of her cottage, where she could become calm.

Dr Laforge sat by her. 'Not the way I expected to meet my new doctor,' he said. 'I thought that we'd agree a time for you to come to the surgery, that I'd introduce you to everyone, show you around and then we could discuss your work. Instead…' he waved a hand at the crashed vehicle '…we meet at an emergency.'

'I remembered that you lived very near. And although I thought that I could cope, I knew that two doctors would be better than one.'

She was not going to let him think that she had called him out of panic and desperation.

'Of course, you were quite right. But now, Dr Blackman, may I formally welcome you to France and to the practice?' He smiled, held out his hand to her.

She took it. His grip was firm but not excessive. Good, a man who didn't need to demonstrate his bodily strength to every attractive female.

'I'm looking forward to working with you,' she said. 'I hope to be as useful a doctor as Dr Cameron.'

'I'm sure you will be. I took you on Dr Cameron's recommendation, he spoke very highly of you.'

She wasn't quite sure about something. So far Dr Laforge had been courteous, perfectly polite, there wasn't a thing he'd said that she could object to. But there seemed to be a reserve about him that she couldn't understand. As if he resented her in some way. And that wasn't right! He was getting a part-time, skilled, English- and French-speaking doctor for what was a comparatively small salary. Not that that was important, she had money. But as Joe Cameron's locum she had expected a warmer welcome.

'Perhaps you would have been happier with a male locum, Dr Laforge?'

That hurt him! She saw the way his mouth hardened, his eyes grow suddenly narrower. But his voice was calm as he said, 'Not at all. In many ways a female doctor will be more use. You will be dealing with a large number of British holidaymakers, mainly families. Almost invariably the children come in with their mothers. Perhaps a woman doctor is better for them.'

'I see,' Kelly said. She still felt there was some tiny touch of prejudice in the doctor. But whether it was the fact that she was British, or the fact that she was a woman, she still didn't know.

When he spoke again his voice was perhaps a little more friendly. 'I saw you comforting the girls,' he said. 'That was a difficult job and you are not even a native French speaker. But your French is excellent.'

'I spent a year in France when I was sixteen. And I met and worked with French soldiers when I was on duty abroad.'

He nodded. 'I read that in your CV, which was very impressive.'

Kelly said nothing. She knew it was impressive.

'So you managed to calm the girls. That was good.'

She managed to shrug. 'Just part of the job.'

'An important part of the job. I think… Perhaps too many doctors disregard the mind. The mind is as important as the body. But because it does not bleed, it does not break, it is easy to think that it does not matter.'

'I used to think that way,' Kelly said forcefully. 'Then I found that my opinion changed.'

Perhaps she had spoken a little too forcefully, given away a little of something about herself. She was aware that the French doctor had turned to look at her, was studying her thoughtfully. 'I understand that and I sympathise,' he said.

So far she had only glanced at him, keeping her eyes fixed on the ground between her feet. But now she looked at him directly. With a slight shock, she realised that he was a very attractive man. Then there was a larger shock—how long had it been since she found any man attractive? Why should she start with this one? And one who seemed to have doubts about her—though she still didn't know why.

She guessed he was about her age—early thirties. He was dressed casually, a dark blue T-shirt, white cotton jeans and espadrilles over bare feet. She wondered if he was going boating. Whatever, the outfit did nothing but enhance a broad-shouldered, obviously muscular body.

His face was pleasant without being excessively good looking. More importantly, it was mobile—she had seen it flick from thoughtful to happy in a half second. Was that a good thing for a doctor? Having everyone able to see instantly what you were thinking? She decided that probably he had learned to mask his feelings when it was necessary.

'You are to work for me for three months, Dr Blackman. I hope you enjoy your stay—but do you have any plans after that? Perhaps a permanent job in France?'

This was getting a little personal. Usually she would have backed away from answering the question. Now she realised that she wouldn't mind answering this particular man—except that she had no answer. 'My plans are a little vague at the moment. I'll just have to see what turns up.'

She wondered if this wasn't a particularly impressive answer. Doctors of her age usually had a very clear idea of what they wanted to do next. A lack of ambition was unusual. So she went on, 'I'm not going back into the army, I'm looking for something new. Some job where my particular skills would be useful. I'm thinking of applying for a job in New Zealand.'

She looked warily at the doctor. He was obviously considering her answer and she had that thought again that he was seeing far more than he revealed. But his next comment surprised her and made her feel defensive.

'You will enjoy your stay in Riom, Dr Blackman. You

will not be lonely. The village is popular with the English, there are many of them here for you to visit.'

She answered without thinking. 'So I believe. And I'm ready for more company—I've been a bit solitary for a while.'

'Sometimes solitude is a gift. At times I…'

Another vehicle drew up in front of them, two men in uniform got out. Dr Laforge sighed. 'And now more paperwork. I spend half my life filling in forms, now I see we will have to fill in a few more. Well, it has to be done. I think we both had—'

'Dr Laforge, am I really needed here? As you said, I'm not even insured yet. Could you take care of all the paperwork?'

He looked at her curiously. 'Of course, if you wish. But people may want to thank you, they will be curious who was so helpful.'

'Doing the job was thanks enough.' Kelly scrambled to her feet. 'We'll have to meet formally later. Shall I phone you on Monday—perhaps arrange a time when I can come and look around the surgery?'

The doctor rose to his feet too. 'As you wish.' Again, he held out his hand. 'Dr Blackman, I look forward to working with you.'

Kelly shook his hand, turned and left.

For a moment Luc watched as she walked down the road. She moved well, her legs striding like an athlete's, like someone who was accustomed to walking. He thought he liked the way she moved.

He shrugged, turned to deal with the officials. Now there would be no end of forms to fill in.

But as he worked with them, his thoughts kept returning to Dr Kelly Blackman. It was unlike him to think so much about a woman he had just met and usually he considered that he had had his fill of Englishwomen. Or of one Englishwoman. He knew it was foolish to generalise.

He also knew that he could have been more welcoming. And Dr Blackman had felt this, had reacted to it. Now he felt slightly guilty. Dr Kelly Blackman had impressed him.

Dr Joe Cameron was a semi-retired British doctor who came to Brittany every summer, lived in his little whitewashed cottage and worked part time at the Merveille surgery. In summer the population of Merveille doubled—mostly with British holidaymakers. Having an English doctor made things so much easier in the surgery.

This summer Joe was going to visit his son in New Zealand. But he had said he just happened to know of the perfect replacement and Luc had trusted Joe's judgement. He hadn't wanted an English woman doctor but Joe had said this one was perfect for the job. Was she too perfect? Luc wondered.

Her looks, for a start. He was accustomed to women who made an effort, who would never be seen without make-up, whose hair was always well arranged, whose dress sense was impeccable. Kelly was none of these. She was dressed simply in shorts and a thin black sweater, walking boots on her feet. Her hair was dark, curly, cropped close to her head. Her face was entirely free of make-up. But…figure and face were both the stuff of dreams. He could close his eyes, see her moving…that was it! She looked like a woman who was happy in her body, who was strong and fit.

He didn't think about women like this! Not now!

'Now, your signature here, Doctor. Are you all right? That is the third mistake you have made.'

'I am sorry. I was working late last night.' Luc jerked himself back to reality. In France, if a doctor couldn't fill in forms, then what good was he?

Somehow, he managed to complete the rest of the paperwork without more trouble, but then, as he strolled back to his car, he thought of Kelly again. For the past year he had been uninterested in women. He remembered an English saying that his ex-wife had used, one that had irritated him no end. *Been there, done that, got the T-shirt.* What did it mean? Whatever it meant, when it came to women, Luc now had a drawer full of T-shirts.

But he couldn't stop thinking of Kelly. There had been nothing that either of them had said that could make him think this way. Their conversation had been formal, stilted even. They weren't even on first-name terms. But he had felt that perhaps there was some kind of affinity between them. Something to do with the way he had seen her glance at him, something to do with the way that she had been happy for him to hold her hand a little longer than was strictly necessary. But she was cautious, she would not let herself be natural. What was it? The avoidance of intimacy, the wariness in her eyes. But also so much competence in her own work! Kelly had some kind of secret, some load of…guilt? Or hurt? He didn't know what. But he intended to find out.

Then he wondered why.

Of course, he knew why she had left the army, why she had been on sick leave. But he had been told—and now believed—that she was over it. Her fear, whatever it was, didn't come from her military career or the illness that had followed it.

But why was he so interested?

He shrugged, angry at himself. To him, Dr Kelly Blackman was just another doctor. She was an attractive woman—but he was not interested in attractive women. Look where it had got him!

As she walked away from the accident, Kelly realised she was fully cured. Six months ago she would have been tempted to break into a run. Anything to get away. But now she was comfortable with her usual fast walk. She could feel some tension in her shoulders—but that was understandable. It was a while since she'd practised emergency medicine. And she thought she'd done well.

Next week she would start work, she decided. It would be her first job in a year. She had no worries about it. She would be dressed in a white coat, have a stethescope round her neck, have a desk between her and whoever she was talking to. She wouldn't be a person. She'd be a doctor. And she now knew she could do that quite easily. If she needed friends, then she could choose them.

She had only been there for a week but the cottage had never seemed so welcoming. She kept the shutters closed in the living room, but the sun eased its way through the slats so there were lines of brightness across the stone floor. She loved it here, it was almost like a home to her. Time to be English, she thought. I'll make myself some tea.

So she made some tea, sticking to the rules she had decided on. The rules weren't really needed now, she didn't need the order in her life. But she'd decided she liked the precision in them.

There was no wandering around the kitchen, mug of tea in hand, teabag still in the mug. Instead, a tray with a small cloth. A cup and saucer, not a mug. A teapot, milk jug, sugar basin—not that she ever took sugar. And a biscuit barrel and a plate for her biscuit. Silly really, she knew. But the ritual was important. And never eat or drink standing up!

She sat on the couch, put the tray on the coffee-table and thought about what had happened earlier. And it was strange! She didn't think of the accident, of the little girls who could have been injured, She thought of Dr Laforge.

She had watched him at work, he was calm, confident of his own efficiency. And he had liked the work, he liked relieving pain. Never mind that, what had he meant to her? For the first time in months she felt that she could imagine being close to a man. Being close that way. Not just any man, but this one. She had felt the first traces of attraction and she knew that he had felt as she did. She wondered how such a feeling could be possible when they had said so little to each other. But she knew it was there.

She shivered. She knew that half her life was now fine. She was cured. But could you be cured of love—or rather the pain that it could bring? That half of her life was still disturbed. Perhaps it was time she should start thinking of her future. She had to have one. She remembered that when she had been on her walk earlier that day she had known that she had got over her illness but she now had to get over Gary. Putting him behind her was hard.

For some reason she thought of Gary and of Luc Laforge. Put them side by side, compared them. They couldn't be more different. For a start, Gary was better looking. Incredibly good looking. People in the streets turned to look at him. As he well knew. But Luc was…well, the more she thought of him, remembered him, the better he became.

Luc seemed to be calm. Life with Gary had to be one long round of excitement. Gary could never be bored. Perhaps it was part of being an actor. Living with him had been energising but exhausting.

Gary had dropped her, cruelly, suddenly, because he'd said he couldn't cope—which had been a lie. She had no idea how Luc would behave if he and she were together. But she suspected that he would do better than Gary.

This was not a good line of thought. Perhaps she had moped long enough, she needed more exercise. She would go for another cliff-top walk.

She walked for three hours, not stopping once. On and off she thought of Luc, wondering how she would work with him.

Yes, she thought she did want to see him again. Just out of curiosity, of course.

Then, thoroughly tired, back to her cottage. A simple evening meal—she never bothered to cook anything too complex—but carefully prepared and properly served. A bowl of home-made vegetable soup. Bread, cheese and salad. An apple and a pear. All ingredients bought from the local market. And a glass of red wine.

She sat in her living room with cloth on the table and napkin in her lap. It was important to do things properly. Live one day at a time.

Half an hour to fill before bedtime. She picked up a folder, leafed through the contents. There was a filled in application form and details of a job in New Zealand. Joe had suggested it to her. She'd never been to New Zealand but had always fancied it. And this was a good job—a peripatetic A and E doctor. The work would be hard but enjoyable. She'd be in the open air, plenty of travel, there'd be skiing, climbing, sailing. The salary was good—and she had all the qualifications asked for, and more. The starting date was in four months' time.

Kelly thought a minute then nodded. Time for decisions now. She tucked the application form into an envelope, sealed it.

Then to bed. Her last thought was that today her life had changed in some way. Then she slept peacefully.

CHAPTER TWO

THE French baker opened very early. Every morning Kelly would walk the quarter mile down to the bakery, buy a baguette and then return for a breakfast of bread, jam from the local market and coffee. Usually taken on the little terrace at the back of the cottage, it was something she really enjoyed. It was one of the rituals that made her enjoy her new life. She didn't like change.

However, this morning was to be different. Just as she was finishing breakfast her phone rang and she looked at it thoughtfully. A phone call meant trouble. The only person who knew she was here was Joe, and there was no good reason for him to ring her.

But it wasn't Joe.

'Dr Blackman, Dr Laforge here. I hope I'm not disturbing you, calling so early?'

For a moment she couldn't speak. He was the last person she had expected to call. But then it struck her…why not? He was to be her employer, there were things they had to discuss before she started work. 'Not at all, Dr Laforge. I'm an early riser anyway. What can I do for you?' She hadn't meant to sound so blunt, so unwelcoming. But the call had come as a shock.

Fortunately, he didn't seem to mind. But his voice was a little uncertain as he continued, 'Well, we'll have to arrange a meeting at the surgery later in the week. But I was wondering if I might call on you, perhaps some time this afternoon. Not to talk about medical matters but to welcome you to the area. And to tell you more about yesterday's accident when you did so well. And it so happens that I have a little something for you.'

A welcome to the area? Something for her? She was intrigued. Whatever could it be?

She knew no one locally, had not yet gone out of her way to make friends. Did she want a caller? Especially a man as attractive as Dr Luc Laforge? Still...he was to be her boss. This could be seen as just a professional courtesy. 'That sounds very nice,' she said, 'and I'd like you to call. When would suit you best?'

'Please! I have invited myself, you must pick the time.'

'Why don't you come about half past three? To a very English afternoon tea? You do drink tea? You're not a completely coffee man?'

'I think English tea is one of the great gifts your country has given the world. I love it. So I'll see you at half past three?'

'I'm looking forward to it,' Kelly said, and rang off.

This was something new to think about. She found that her coffee-pot was cold, decided to percolate just one cup more. She walked to the kitchen, frowned as she ran water into the percolator.

Dr Luc Laforge wanted to call on her. He wasn't coming

here to talk about work, he had a mysterious present for her. But she knew that there was more to him coming than that.

There had been that awareness, that shiver of knowledge between them. He was a man, she was a woman. For a moment something had reached out from each of them. It had been a slight, tentative feeling. But there had been a strength to it that had surprised her. Each had found the other attractive. She wanted to know more about this man. To see if their very different personalities could have something in common.

Then she laughed, without much humour. She had been caught this way before, had learned a bitter lesson. So she wanted there to be nothing between her and this man but a professional relationship. She wanted there to be nothing between her and any man.

Still…behind her she could hear the percolator starting to bubble. The cheerful sound made her spirits rise. Perhaps, soon, she could bubble too.

He was calling that afternoon. A young gentleman—well, youngish—calling on a young—well, youngish—lady. It all seemed very Jane Austen. Perhaps it would be more proper if she had a chaperone! A chaperone! For a woman who had been through what she had! Kelly giggled. Then she thought. It had been too long since she had managed to giggle. Perhaps things were looking up.

Had afternoon tea been the right thing to offer him? She hadn't thought what might be suitable, the idea of afternoon tea had just emerged. Anyway, in the middle of the afternoon she couldn't offer alcohol. And not a full meal either—they were not on lunch or dinner terms yet. She had decided to be soundly English, offer him tea. Perhaps she'd better get back down to the baker's and buy a selection of cakes. They were gorgeous.

Next problem. What to wear? Jeans or shorts and T-shirt or sweater were all very well, but something told her that he would not come dressed casually. She needed a dress but then blanched as she thought of her wardrobe. She had come here to relax, to work part time in the surgery, to be simply her own self. A social life had been the last thing she had expected. So…she had suitable clothes for working in, suitable clothes for walking in, but the only thing vaguely smart was one summer dress. A white one. And that would need ironing, she'd never taken it out of her case.

What about make-up? And then she did laugh. All she had used for the last few months had been sunblock. And that had been quite sufficient. But now…perhaps she would make a bit of an effort. There was a chemist in the village, she could buy a coral lipstick and some black mascara. And perhaps an expensive scented shampoo.

She was almost looking forward to this visit. She wondered why.

Luc blinked. This was a different woman! No, she was not different, she was the same woman he had thought of all night. But she was different.

Her face was as beautiful as ever, her body just as supple, as rounded. So what had changed? Not much, he realised. A very feminine white dress, just a touch of make-up and a slightly different hairstyle. What was different was her attitude. Before she had been the complete professional, concerned only with her work. But now she was a woman, not a doctor.

'Do come in, Dr Laforge. It's not too warm, I thought we might have tea on the terrace. You did mean it when you said you liked tea?'

'I did. Tea would be most pleasant.' He stepped into her living room, took a hand from behind his back. 'I've brought you some flowers. They are from my garden.' He handed her a bunch of roses in shades of red and yellow.

'They're lovely! And from your own garden! Dr Laforge, how good of you.'

He saw that her delight was genuine and it pleased him. 'I don't have much time to garden myself,' he said. 'I have to say that my gardener is responsible for these.'

'But you brought them. Come through to the terrace and I'll put them in water.'

He followed her through the living room. He had been in the cottage before, visiting Joe. And it interested him to notice that the living room was entirely unchanged. Dr Blackman had made no effort to imprint her own character on the room. If anything, she appeared to have gone to some trouble to keep it exactly as it had been. Yes, interesting.

He recognised that she was a bird of passage, ready to fly when her time was done.

He thought she was a woman who would recognise, would respond to signs. So he wasn't wearing his usual, non-professional casual clothes. He wore a light grey linen suit, a dark blue silk shirt. He wanted to appear as a man who had thought about the woman he was visiting, who saw this visit as an important one. When she had opened the door to him he had noticed the way her eyes had flicked over him, then the guarded expression of approval.

She led him to the terrace, where two chairs and a table

waited ready for them. 'If you would like to wait here a minute I'll see to the flowers and fetch the tea. I have it all ready.'

He knew better than to offer to help. Well, on the first visit anyway.

She served the tea with some formality and he appreciated it. A proper teapot, cups and saucers, a plate of cakes. She asked him how he liked it, poured the tea, offered him a cake and then the niceties were over. What were they to talk about?

He had decided as he'd driven here that there was something that had to be settled at once.

'I very much like English tea,' he said. 'For some time I was married to an English girl and…well, it all ended nastily. We are now divorced. For me, the only good thing to come out of it was my daughter and a taste for tea.'

'I see. A divorce from an English girl. When you met an English woman yesterday, was that why you were less than pleased?'

He winced. He hadn't realised that he was so transparent. 'Possibly so. If that is how I appeared then I must apologise. I should not be prejudiced. And I saw quickly that you were a very efficient doctor.' He paused and then said meaningfully, 'Dr Blackwood.'

She laughed at that. 'You feel that by now we should have gone beyond formality? Then call me Kelly and I will call you Luc.' She leaned over, offered him her hand.

'Good to meet you, Kelly.' A warm hand, a firm grip. He didn't want to let go and he wondered if she felt the same. But…whatever this was, this should be taken slowly. For the moment keep things casual, light-hearted. After all, he didn't even know what he wanted! 'As ever, your English tea is superb,' he said. 'But I detect that the cakes are French. From our local *boulangerie*.'

'And very fine they are. But if my mother had known you were coming to tea she would have baked you scones. You've had English scones?'

'Well, yes.'

Kelly laughed again. 'Your lack of enthusiasm is obvious. But I can assure you that the Blackman scones are good.'

'Then I would like to try them. Perhaps next time?'

This was only meant to be a single visit, just a welcome to her. But now he had indicated that he wanted to call again. How would she react? He could tell that she realised the importance of what he had just suggested. 'Perhaps,' she said. Well, that was better than nothing.

He decided to move onto safer topics. 'I want to tell you a little about the accident,' he said. 'First, no one was seriously hurt. All the girls but one are now out of hospital. But secondly…the one little girl still in hospital is the one who was concussed. Whose head was bleeding so badly. Your bandaging turned what could have been a dangerous injury into one that was just serious. Both the hospital staff and myself were very impressed. You could tell this is the kind of work you've done before.'

Her reply was more shocking because it came out so casually. 'As a field doctor in the army, sometimes I had to work in an actual field.'

He recognised her confidence. This woman knew her own worth.

'Of course, we doctors come across a variety of problems. Anyway, the headmistress of the school asked me to give you her thanks in person. Those thanks I do give. Now, on to more tedious matters.'

He fumbled in his pocket, took out a sheaf of papers. 'I suspect that British beaurocracy is as awkward as French beaurocracy. I spent more time filling in forms about that accident than we spent dealing with it. But I have to ask you again. The headmistress asked me to submit a bill for what I did. In fact, she demanded that I submit a bill. And she says you too are entitled to payment.'

'If there has to be payment, you have it or let the school keep it.' She smiled wryly. 'As you pointed out, I am not yet insured to practise medicine in France.'

'I will pass on your message. So, business over. Please, may I have more tea?' He was enjoying his drink.

They chatted for a few minutes more, talking easily, happily. Then he knew he had to go, he had calls to make, things to do. He stood, and as he did so there was a knock at the door. Kelly went to answer it, came back with a thick packet liberally covered with stamps. 'My mail,' she said. 'When I was out yesterday, my neighbour next door took it in for me. Dr Cameron collects it, sends it on in bulk. Excuse me a minute. There's a journal he said he'd send me.'

She pulled at the packet edge, spilled letters, cards and wrapped magazines onto the table. First, he saw her reach for a journal—but as she did so her wrist brushed a letter into sight. It seemed just an ordinary letter—but the address was written in green ink.

He heard her gasp. He looked at her face. Suddenly it was white. For the moment he was forgotten, he saw her grab the letter, tear it open. There was just one sheet of paper inside—also written in green ink. She read it. Then her eyes closed and she grasped the table for support.

He thought to move round, perhaps to hold and comfort her. Then something told him that that was the last thing that she needed.

Her eyes opened. Unfocussed, she looked at him and he could tell that it took her a while to realise who he was. Then she slumped into her chair. He looked at her a moment longer, then found his way into her kitchen, fetched her a glass of water. 'This might help,' he said.

She drank the water. Then she shook her head, obviously trying to get a grip of her whirling emotions.

'You have had bad news,' Luc said. 'Is there any way I can help or would it be better if I left you alone?'

'Perhaps you had better go now. Thank you for calling, Dr Laforge.'

So he was Dr Laforge again. 'Could I call again? Perhaps tomorrow?'

'I don't think there's much point. We'll have to work together but I believe it is probably best to keep social life and professional life separate. Goodbye, Dr Laforge.'

'Goodbye, Dr Blackman…Kelly. I trust you will be well soon. I'll let myself out.'

Just before he closed the door he looked back at her. She was crouched in her chair, tearing the letter into pieces… smaller and smaller pieces until there were only tiny fragments left. He sighed. He wanted to go back, to help her, comfort her. But he knew it would be no use.

Kelly sat motionless for the next half-hour, eyes clenched shut, shoulders hunched, hands clasped in her lap. Then she opened her eyes, looked around her. The sun shone, there was a breeze bringing countryside scents into her garden, somewhere a bird sang. And around the feet of her chair were scattered fragments of paper—some showing the tell-tale green ink.

Gary's full name was Gary Green. He had always written his letters with green ink, he thought it made people remember him. What a stupid idea!

The tiny scraps looked like confetti, she thought. The stuff people threw around at weddings. She had thought that when she married Gary, they would have had confetti thrown at them. Not any more.

They had been going to get married. She'd worn the en-gagement ring, they had booked the church, organised the reception, had been making a list of guests. All right, she hadn't been herself, she had still been ill. But she would soon have recovered. And if Gary had been ill she would have stood by him. But Gary hadn't been up to that. So they had broken up, finally, irrevocably, three months ago. Three short months! And now Gary had written to say he had found another fiancée, they were engaged, going to get married quite soon. He thought Kelly ought to know. Three months! Was that all that the memory of their love was worth?

And this message had come just as her life was on an even keel again, when there might be a hope of happiness for her. Happiness? She'd settle for normality. So what should she do? She'd fight on.

Work was the answer. She fetched brush and pan, swept up the remains of Gary's letter and dropped them in the fireplace. Then she set light to them. Let them disappear into smoke.

She checked the other contents of her packet from Joe—
nothing of great importance.

Then there were the tea dishes to clear away. After that
she would go for another walk—a good long lonely one,
ten miles at least. The fatigue afterwards always made her
feel better.

But as she was clearing away, something struck her. She
had told Luc that there was no point in them meeting again
until she started work. Just the opposite of what she had
been going to say before the letter had arrived. Why should
Gary be the one to make her change her mind about things?
And she had acted towards Luc…well, gracelessly would
be one way of putting it. Rudely would be another. She was
her own woman now. She would put things right with him.

The walk did improve her mood. Perhaps she was getting
better. So as soon as she had showered and changed she took
Luc's card from where she had placed it on the mantelshelf.
A moment of indecision. Then she phoned him on his mobile.

'Dr Laforge…Luc? It's…it's Kelly.'

His reply was warm, eager. 'Kelly! How are you? I'm
so glad you phoned. I was worried about you.'

'I'm sorry about that. A bit of my past came up to haunt
me and I'm afraid I took it out of you. I'm phoning to
apologise, I'm not usually so unpleasant.'

'You weren't being unpleasant. You were hurt, I could
tell. You felt that nobody in the entire world was worth
bothering about, that when you thought you were getting
over things, they suddenly got worse again. And that was
the last straw.'

Kelly was intrigued. 'That's exactly right. How did you
know that?'

It was a moment before he answered. 'I've been there myself, sometimes I think I still am there. Do I take it that it was a letter from an ex-lover?'

'We were engaged. He broke it off. Now he writes to say that he's soon going to get married. Only three months after our break-up!'

Luc's voice was sympathetic. 'There's more, isn't there? You try to persuade yourself that he was not worth the trouble, that you're well rid of him, that you'll do better next time. And then you remember one of those perfect days you spent together and you're inconsolable again.'

'Right,' said Kelly. How did he know her thoughts so well? She was intrigued. But now came what she had thought would be the hard part—but, in fact, she now didn't feel too bad about it. 'Luc, I told you that there was no point in you calling again, but if you'd like ever to call round again—as a friend—you'd be very welcome. You didn't even get to finish your tea.'

'I'd love that! Is tomorrow afternoon too soon? Say, about three again?'

'Not at all. I'd be pleased to see you.' The idea made her both embarrassed and excited.

'Just one thing, then. Since you've got plenty of notice, any chance of me trying one of the scones your mother was famous for?'

'I think it could be arranged,' she said.

Luc put down the phone and smiled and then frowned. What was he doing? He was happy because of the invitation, he wanted to see more of Kelly. He was not quite sure why. She was a very attractive woman—he enjoyed her company. He could persuade himself that all he was doing was welcoming a colleague to the neighbourhood. But… when his wife had finally left him he had decided that women were not for him. They only brought heartbreak. He would live with and for his daughter, they would be happy together.

So why was he looking forward so much to meeting Kelly again?

CHAPTER THREE

KELLY answered the phone the next morning and when she heard Luc's voice she was worried at once. What if he couldn't come? Then she wondered why she was so worried about a man she had barely met.

'Kelly—perhaps I'd better call you Dr Blackman—I have a favour to ask you.'

'Yes?' Kelly said carefully. She didn't want to rush into anything. She wasn't yet sure what kind of relationship she wanted to have with Luc. She had learned to be cautious.

'I've had a phone call from a woman who lives in Riom. She lives very close to you—about a kilometre away. She says her fourteen-year-old son has bruised his chest and is having difficulty breathing and she wants me to come out to see him. Now, we're busy today. I know the family, both mother and son exaggerate their troubles. I've been called out at midnight because the son was having a bad coughing fit.'

'You want me to go down there and deal with the problem,' Kelly guessed.

'Just decide if I'm really needed. Then I'll come if necessary.'

'That's no problem at all, but am I insured?'

There was a smile in his voice as he replied, 'In fact, you are insured. I arranged it this morning.'

'Right. I'll be there in half an hour. What's the address?'

She realised that she felt a bit excited at the prospect of acting like a real doctor, not someone reacting to an emergency. It would be another step forward. She dressed in what she thought was a suitable doctor's outfit. Then she fetched her doctor's bag. It was brand-new, she had bought it, stocked it before coming to France. It was so different from the army medical kit she used to have. There were no dressings for gunshot wounds for a start!

She felt quite pleased with herself as she walked the small distance to the address she had been given. She was helping Luc. And she felt confident.

Madame Ducasse was worried about her son Etienne. She was a widow, he was her only son, he was a sickly boy but also difficult, and was Madame Blackman sure that she was a doctor and not just a nurse? Etienne really needed a doctor. And she was not sure how he would react to a lady examining him. She herself, his mother, had not been able to see what was the matter. She had such trouble with him…

'Where is he?' interrupted Kelly.

She followed the still explaining Madame Ducasse up the stairs, already half-convinced that the only thing wrong with Etienne was his mother. But when she opened the bedroom door and heard the laboured breathing, she knew she was wrong. Etienne was not faking.

'Hi, Etienne, I'm Dr Blackman. Now, tell me what happened.'

'Nothing happened. This just sort of started.' Etienne was a poor liar.

'I need to examine your son,' Kelly told Mrs Ducasse. 'Please wait downstairs, I will speak to you later.'

Mrs Ducasse obviously didn't think this a good idea. But Kelly had years of experience to draw on. In a sickroom, what she wanted she got. Mrs Ducasse left. Kelly looked at her patient, sized him up.

'Possibly I won't have to tell your mother all the details,' she said, 'but you have to tell me. Now, what happened?'

A short but typical story. On his way to school Etienne had been mixing with older boys his mother thought he shouldn't be mixing with in a place he shouldn't have been either. A derelict house. There had been some horseplay, some pushing, and Etienne had fallen onto his side. And it hurt. So he had come straight home.

'Let's have a look at you,' Kelly said. 'I'll listen to your chest first.'

The wheeze was getting worse. There was no sound from one side of the chest. Kelly realised the lung had deflated. Fingertip gently, she felt Etienne's ribs. There! One was broken.

She knew what had happened, she had dealt with this often. It was a common injury among soldiers thrown about when an armoured vehicle was attacked and crashed.

Etienne had a pneumothorax. A broken rib had punctured the lung wall so that air was escaping out of the lung into the pleural cavity—the space between the chest wall and the lung lining. If not treated, the consequences could be serious.

She went out of the bedroom and phoned Luc. 'Luc, the patient has a broken rib and a pneumothorax.'

Silence for a minute at the other end of the line. 'So

much for jumping to conclusions and diagnosing by phone,' he said. 'I should have known better.'

'Having met Madame Ducasse, I think that your diagnosis was very reasonable. Luc, I can handle this but ideally Etienne should be in hospital for a couple of days. If you like, I'll aspirate the chest and put a temporary drain in. I have the kit.'

'Good idea. I'll arrange for him to be picked up by ambulance and brought here. Dr Blackman, welcome to the practice.'

'It's a pleasure to join it.'

She walked back home a little later feeling more contented than she had been for a while. Life was looking up!

It was weird, how much her mood changed when she got back to the cottage, started thinking about the afternoon. She was not the steely, competent doctor she had just been. Kelly hadn't felt this way in years—not since she was a teenager. Sort of fluttery, and agitated.

It had taken a special visit to the village shop to buy the ingredients. And then there was the tussle with the oven of the gas stove. She hadn't done much cooking in this oven, And no baking at all. A good thing that she had over-bought ingredients. Two batches of scones had to be thrown to the birds before she got them exactly right. But then she thought her mother would be proud of them. And with Breton butter, cream and jam…well, the French weren't the only people who could bake well.

She moved a dozen times from living room to terrace, re-arranging things, checking that all was well, looking again at herself in the big mirror. Was her hair all right? Her make-up not smudged? Most important, were the scones still okay?

And that settled it. She was being ridiculous! What could go wrong with a scone once it was baked?

There was no problem with a dress. She only had the one so she had to wear it again. But she wrapped a red silk scarf loosely round her neck.

There was a knock on the door, exactly at three. She made herself move to answer it in a normal way.

Her heart thumped when she saw him on the doorstep. It hadn't done that for quite a while. She knew that later she'd have to ask herself why. He was dressed differently this time but still obviously with some care. A lightweight blue summer jacket over a white shirt. No tie again—well, it was high summer. And the whiteness of his shirt emphasised his tanned, muscular neck.

'Luc—it's good to see you.'

'It's good to see you too. You obviously feel better. No flowers today, but I did bring a present. I must add it's not from me.'

He handed her a parcel, carefully wrapped in gold paper. 'With the compliments and thanks of Madame La Salle, the headmistress of L'École Élémentaire de Merveille.'

'A surprise present! Can I open it now? I haven't had a surprise present in years.'

'Of course you can.'

'Well, come through to the terrace and I'll do it there.' She felt excited, like a child.

First, the gold paper, then a stout cardboard box and tissue paper. And finally… 'How lovely! It's a bottle of champagne.

'But you deserve it as much as me. In fact, you did more than me. It's too early to drink now but perhaps one evening we could…' Her voice faltered as she realised what she was saying. 'Perhaps we could drink it together.'

He had obviously noted her sudden embarrassment but pretended not to. 'That would be very pleasant. But now I have another gift—a letter.' He handed her a rather bulky envelope.

Kelly opened it, took out a large sheet of paper and smiled when she saw what was on it. 'Luc, this is lovely too! It's a letter from the girls we helped. Perhaps with a little assistance here and there. I've never had a letter in red crayon before. They thank me for helping them and say that now they all want to be doctors. And they've drawn me a picture.'

She handed him the letter. 'A nice letter but with just a little bit of artistic license.' He grinned. 'I don't remember the flames being anything like as high.'

'It doesn't matter. I'm going to pin it on the kitchen wall.'

She found herself curiously at home with Luc. She didn't feel threatened, or angry or depressed. She liked being with him and it was just the man himself. Of course, there was a faint frisson of sexual excitement—the first she had felt for months now. But that wasn't the main cause of her pleasure. Not yet, a tiny voice inside her whispered. But she ignored it.

'I'll fetch the tea now,' she said. 'Sit here and enjoy the sun. I won't be a moment.' In fact, she needed a moment alone to get control over her thoughts and feelings. She seemed to be making some kind of progress—but progress to where? She couldn't quite tell her mood—was she afraid or excited?

She now knew she was definitely attracted to Luc. It was exciting—but look where excitement had got her before. Too involved with Gary.

Gary had been the great love of her life—in effect, the only love of her life. She had offered her love to him without question, and when he'd rejected her she'd had no experience to draw on to help her. She was left with just one idea. She would never allow herself to be drawn into this kind of situation again. Love wasn't for her.

Was that true? She'd have to think. Not now. Now was the time for tea.

The Blackman scones were considered a great success. 'As good as any Frenchwoman could bake,' Luc announced, 'if she tried, that is.'

'French women don't bake,' Kelly pointed out. 'Like me, they go to the *boulangerie* for cakes.'

'That is true. But I have to say that the scones were… enhanced by the addition of Breton cream and butter and French jam.'

'Point taken,' said Kelly. How long had it been since she'd had a gentle, joking conversation like this? 'Do have another one,' she said.

For a while there was little conversation. They drank tea, finished the scones; he told her the French names of a couple of birds that were singing in the garden. Both knew that something had grown between them, a feeling that neither of them fully understood. A feeling that had to be acknowledged.

Finally she cleared away the tea-tray, refusing his offer of help. When she came back to the terrace she pushed the table to one side, moved her chair so that they were sitting side by side. For a while she didn't want to be sitting opposite him, where they would have to look into each other's eyes.

'Will Dr Cameron be visiting soon?' Luc asked, apparently casually. 'You'll be made very welcome, of course, but Joe will be missed in the surgery.'

'He said he'd come over before he went to New Zealand. I think he wants to check in on me before he flies halfway round the world.'

'He is a good friend, he spoke very highly of you,' Luc commented.

'I've known Joe Cameron a long time,' she said. 'When I was young he was a neighbour. He was still in the army then but when he was home I'd go to his house and he'd coach me for my science exams. Knowing him was one reason why I wanted to be a doctor. And once I'd been accepted at medical school I joined the army, just like Joe had done. They sponsored me through my course.'

'And you're proud of that. I can tell.'

'Yes. I am proud.'

She knew he must have more questions, wondered how he would put them. As ever, it was with delicacy.

'Yesterday I noticed that you had a scar on your leg. Did you get that on active service? Please, if you don't want to talk about it, that is fine. We can talk about something else.'

'I don't mind talking about it,' she said. 'I can now live quite happily with the memories and feelings that I used to try to suppress. They're part of my life, I accept them.'

She paused a moment, she knew she was taking a bold step. 'And…for some reason I want you to know all the details.'

He reached across, stroked the back of her hand, which was resting on the arm of her chair. Just a slight touch of his fingertips, but it brought her much pleasure.

'Tell me what you can,' he said, 'I want to…know you.'

'Right. First thing is, the leg injury is largely unimportant. It was a piece of shrapnel, a white-hot chunk of metal from a mortar shell that tore away a lump of flesh. No bone damage and now I've got complete movement and strength in the leg. No pain, just a scar. I got off lightly.'

'Lightly? I don't think so.'

'Lightly compared to what else I saw. I was in the Middle East, an army surgeon. A badly injured soldier's chance of survival is a hundred per cent greater if he receives treatment in the first hour after being injured. So I was working with a team, in a tent, in temperatures you can only think of in nightmares, with the wind howling and blowing sand into everything. And we were it. No relief team. We were on call night and day. More than once I worked a twenty-four-hour shift. Then I had to stop because I just couldn't see straight.'

'For how long did you do this?'

'For as long as I was needed. We had all served well past the normal tour of duty weeks past. But what do you do if there's no one to replace you?'

'You weren't offered special treatment because you were a woman?'

'Any man who offered it would regret it,' Kelly snarled.

'I could have guessed you'd say that. Tell me more. Will you tell me what finally happened? What was the last thing you just couldn't take?'

'Why d'you think something finally happened?' She tried to make her voice casual, but she knew she didn't succeed.

'Kelly, I'm a doctor, as concerned with the mind as the body. It's obvious something happened to you. But you only have to tell me if you wish.'

There had been such a time. It had been the hardest bit, the time when finally, ultimately, she'd had to give up. Her body, her mind—more than both of these, her spirit just could not take any more. And the shrapnel in her leg hadn't helped.

'Finally, there was one day. There was a bit of a push on, the enemy were getting too close. I operated on seventeen injured men that day. Five of them died. Then, just for five minutes, we came under enemy fire.'

'Not an experience that many doctors can claim.'

She shrugged. 'It was a risk of the job. At the time it affected me, but now that's all over. There was an explosion outside the tent, probably a mortar bomb, and I found myself sitting on the floor with blood streaming from my leg. It didn't hurt. Nothing hurt. But I got carried out and I was on a helicopter half an hour later, headed for base camp.'

She paused a moment, thought about what she had just told him. It was a story she had told too many times before and usually ended with her in tears. But not any more. She felt perfectly calm. Now it was just a distant memory. She had come through it. She knew that.

'And then?' Luc persisted gently.

'Well, my leg was treated. No great problem. Like I said, it's completely cured now. But there was something else broken, my spirit. In the First World War they called it shell shock. Now it has a more professional name—PTSD. Post-traumatic stress disorder. It's not fashionable because there's no apparent injury. No eyes missing, no amputated limbs, no visible scars. But it's there all right. And so I was invalided out of the army a year ago. No stain on my record—in fact, I might even get a medal.'

'And you were placed under the care of Dr Cameron?'

'I was. I suspect he pulled a few strings to get charge of me, but I'm glad he did. I was a year under his care and now I'm completely cured. No more nightmares, no more depression, no more hallucinations. No more shaking hands and body.'

'I know of PTSD. And, believe me, Kelly, I know it is an injury that can hurt as much as any physical complaint. And like so many physical complaints, it can be cured.'

It wasn't at all what she had expected. But it seemed perfectly proper when Luc stretched his arm round her, eased her to him so her head was resting on his shoulder.

'I too have been in battle,' he said. 'And in battle I have seen men huddle together for comfort. So, for a moment, we will be two soldiers and try to forget the troubles round us.'

'That's nice,' she said. But what was she doing? His arm was round her, she had her head tucked into the bend of his arm and shoulder, she could feel the warmth of his body, smell the delicate cologne that he must use. And somewhere there was a pulse, she could sense rather than feel the steady beat. And she liked it! She felt relaxed, comforted, at peace with the world. She hadn't been this way with a man for so long. And why this man? She hardly knew him.

'You say that you were a soldier too?' she asked, half drowsily. 'When was that?'

'Before I studied medicine, when I was a young man, I spent some time in the French army. As a soldier, you understand, not a doctor in any way. I was a medical orderly. I was sent to Africa with a small contingent of men on what was called a peace-keeping operation. A peace-keeping mission! That was a joke!'

He paused, and she could feel the alteration in his mood, could hear the slight agitation in his voice.

'I'm disturbing you, I'm sorry,' she muttered. 'Can you forget it for now?'

'You make it easier for me to forget, Kelly. But I want you to know that I too have suffered a little of what you felt. I can sympathise. Unlike you, though, I was not helping injured men. Mostly I was standing by and watching people kill each other for no apparent reason. Our orders were not to interfere unless attacked, we couldn't be seen to take sides. So we did little or nothing.'

She wasn't relaxed and at peace now, she was fascinated, wanted to know more. 'How did you cope? Did you get PTSD too?'

He shrugged. 'The mission was soon over, we were brought back to France. I left the army and found some peace in work. I started my medical course. Studying was hard but it helped. And now when I look back at those times it is with sadness—but the realisation that I had done all I could. You have to learn to accept what you cannot change and find your own peace.'

Something struck her. 'Luc, are you telling me this as some kind of therapy? Trying to make me feel better? I told you, I'm cured.' She didn't know whether she was pleased or angry at what he was trying to do.

He shook his head. 'Talking about it might be therapy. But it is therapy for me, not you. Every now and again I need to take out my memories, examine them, decide that they are past, dealt with. Then I can lead my happy life again.'

'So I'm helping you?'

'I hope so,' he said. And...he kissed her.

He leaned over and kissed her, just a gentle kiss, a bare touching of his lips on hers. The kind of kiss you might give to a baby on its cheek. But she decided she loved it.

She was shocked, of course. This was the last thing she had expected to happen. Then she was more shocked as he moved backwards, to end the kiss. She wasn't ready for that yet! She liked it! So she put her hand round his neck and pulled his head down to hers, felt his surprise, his tiny resistance, and then the delight as he kissed her again. This time with much more passion. Delicate still. But no one had ever kissed a baby like this. Perhaps if she leaned back a little more he might...

From somewhere there was the ringing of a mobile phone. A harsh, loud, insistent ring, the kind of ring that a doctor's phone might have. And Luc moved away from her, took the phone from his pocket and answered. She could sense his regret.

'Yes, Marie...I could... Why don't people give us some warning?' Then Kelly heard has voice soften. 'Of course I will. We know these things happen... Say a couple hours, then? Fine.' He put the phone back in his pocket.

He turned to Kelly, his expression half sad, half resigned. 'If you're a doctor in the countryside, these thing happen. That was the midwife, Marie Rimbaud. She's just this minute delivered one baby and had a phone call to say that another seems to be due—about three weeks premature. Marie can be there in a couple of hours but until then she asked me to fill in?

'Kelly, right now leaving you is the last thing I want but—'

'But you must,' Kelly said briskly. 'Right, I understand. Can I come with you? Perhaps I could help.'

He looked surprised. 'You want to come with me? Why?'

'I've not had much experience of births in the army— a couple of emergency ones in wrecked buildings—but I think it might be good if I got some more experience.'

'Right. Let's go. The farmhouse is about half an hour away.' He shook his head. 'Home births are fine—until something goes wrong—like now.'

'In medicine you can never plan for everything.'

As they drove off in his car she had to admit to herself that she didn't just want to help. She wanted to stay with Luc. She remembered the old army maxim. *Never volunteer.* Well, she wasn't in the army now.

They drove into the yard of a large and prosperous farmhouse, were ushered inside at once. There was a ground-floor room with a bathroom adjoining, obviously carefully prepared for a home birth.

Cecile was a primigravida. So far all had gone well with her pregnancy, she had been carefully looked after, had followed all instructions exactly. Then she had slipped. Fallen onto the arm of a chair and at first had thought that all was well. However, she had gone to bed, just in case— and then… 'I felt all damp. Dr Laforge, the waters have broken, I've started contractions and I'm not ready yet!'

Luc's voice was kind. 'Babies come in their own time, Cecile. There's no need to worry. Marie will be here shortly, and until then you'll have two doctors. This is another member of our surgery, Dr Blackwood. Now, shall we begin?'

He placed a hand on Cecile's abdomen, looked at his

watch. 'Contractions only five minutes apart. Somebody wants to be born quickly.'

Marie had brought all the necessary sealed packages and boxes, Luc and Kelly prepared everything that might be needed. They put on the scrubs that Marie had thoughtfully left. Then baseline observations. Luc asked Kelly to check and record temperature, blood pressure, pulse and respiration rate. Then he took the Pinard's stethoscope, placed it on Cecile's abdomen and listened to the baby's heart. After a moment he passed the stethoscope to Kelly for her to listen. 'A good healthy heartbeat,' Kelly said. 'Cecile, you're going to have a fine strong baby.'

Luc performed the internal examination. 'Head at plus two,' he reported.

There was gas and air available, but Cecile appeared to not need it. She had practised her relaxation exercises, seemed to be more in control than most mothers-to-be.

After half an hour her husband arrived. He had been on a business trip in Rouen, the family had phoned him. And now he seemed more excited, more concerned, more stressed than the mother-to-be. 'Cecile, are you all right? Are you in pain? Can we get you anything?'

'Guillaume, I am fine! Now, stop worrying!'

While Guillaume was bending over his wife, Kelly saw Luc wink at her, and nod towards the door. She understood at once. 'Guillaume, do you have a minute? We have to check on a couple of things.'

She took Guillaume outside, told him that Cecile needed to rest now and he could do her most good by having a cup of coffee and waiting outside until they called him. 'You will be there for her for the birth. That is vital. But for now be calm.'

No birth could have been simpler. Guillaume was called in. Kelly kept a special eye on him in case he fainted. Luc delivered the baby, handed a perfect little boy to Kelly who wrapped him, and put him onto his mother's breast. Guillaume shook a little, but didn't faint.

Kelly felt that sense of excitement and achievement that midwives spoke of. She glanced at Luc, who obviously felt the same way. Something had happened that they had both shared.

But there were still things to do.

'Shall I take over now?' a voice asked. Marie had arrived.

A job well done but now they weren't needed. Luc was driving her home. Nervously, Kelly said, 'If there isn't anywhere you have to go to, perhaps you'd like to stay for tea. I can cook some—'

His phone rang. Again? Luc had connected his hands-free earpiece and microphone, and answered at once. 'Dr Laforge.' Kelly heard a babble from the earpiece, obviously someone very upset. Eventually Luc said, 'I see… It happened when? No, we can't wait till he gets to hospital, he probably needs an injection at once… Yes, I know I'm not on duty… Yes, of course.'

He clicked off the phone, looked at her. 'Another emergency,' he said. 'But of a different kind. Jean-Paul Lartigue is eighty-four, he has had yet another cardiac episode. I must go.'

'I know. I'm a doctor too, remember.'

'I can drop you off at home first.'

He drove her home, stepped inside her front door, took her hands in his and looked at her. She knew what he was thinking, she felt the same way. They were both wondered what would come next. And perhaps there was a touch of relief. Too much was happening too soon. He released her hands, bent over her, took her head in his hands and kissed her quickly, but so deeply that it left her senses reeling. 'If there is time, may I come back?' he asked.

'I'd like that.'

Then he was gone.

She had left the tea dishes out on the terrace. Kelly mechanically cleared them away, washed everything, put it in its place. She had kept a few scones back wrapped in a packet, which she had intended to give to Luc as he left. Too late now. Or was it?

He had said that he would be back. Was that what she wanted? Or a different question—was that what would be good for her? She didn't know. When she had come to the cottage she had decided, at least for a while, to lead a calm existence. She would practise simple medicine, have a quiet social life, avoid any violent emotional experiences. After three months she would find a job more fitting to her training and character. She blinked. Not doing too well so far.

She had invited Luc back. Why? And when he had kissed her she had—to be brutally honest—loved it. And at the same time felt amazed at herself.

So what was she to do? The memory of Gary's letter came back to her—no way did she need that kind of experience again! She was off men. Should she welcome Luc back, or should she tell him that it had all been an unfortunate mistake, that it would be better if he didn't call again? She knew enough of the man to know that he would accept this without question—even if it hurt him.

She decided to do nothing. Not to do nothing because she didn't dare to make up her mind but because she was curious about what her options were. She had kissed Luc. She had enjoyed it. Now what?

She waited. When it was time she made herself a simple tea, fish and salad, and put enough in the fridge so that if Luc came and wanted to join her there would be no trouble. But he didn't come. Instead, there was a phone call.

His voice was formal. 'Madame Blackman? Dr Laforge here. We had an arrangement. I had intended to call on you later because there are things we have to discuss. But I'm afraid that I have an emergency case here. I doubt that I'll be able to get away for quite some time.'

'That's quite all right, Doctor, I do understand. Phone me when you have time and we'll arrange an appointment.'

'Of course. I am so sorry.' He rang off.

For a moment she was upset. He could have put a little more warmth in his voice. But then she realised. There was probably someone within earshot. This had been a perfect doctor/doctor conversation. Disappointed—but not too much—she wondered when he would call again.

He didn't call again that evening. Then she remembered where he had gone, to see old Jean-Paul Lartigue, who had suffered yet another cardiac episode. Another cardiac episode? Not good. She wondered if Jean-Paul had been too ill to be moved—if Luc was with him even now. She seemed to have gathered that French doctors managed to spend more time at home with their patients than English doctors did.

She had taken up the local French habit of retiring very early and rising very early too. So at ten o'clock she had bathed, put on her nightie and was sitting downstairs in her dressing-gown, having a last ten-minute read.

And her mobile phone rang. That was unusual! A phone call at this time of night. 'Yes?' she answered cautiously.

'Dr Blackman… What am I saying? Kelly, this is Luc. I hope I didn't wake you?'

She paused a moment, thought, and then said deliberately, 'I'm still up, and will be for a little while longer. Did you have a difficult case?'

'Jean-Paul Lartigue. He died, I was with him. He was once a soldier you know, fought in the Second World War. He asked me if I'd arrange for him to be buried in his uniform.'

'I'm so sorry. You sound upset. Was he a friend?'

'We are doctors, we are used to death. But I was brought up to respect Jean-Paul. He was a war hero. He liked me as his doctor because I too had been a soldier.'

'I take it that that means that you are a little upset. So if you have time, would you like to come round for a nightcap? Just a quick one?'

Then she shivered. What had she just said?

'I would like that,' he said slowly, 'but are you sure that I would not be disturbing you?'

Now, that was a foolish question. Of course he would disturb her. But still… 'Not at all,' she lied.

'Then I shall be there in exactly five minutes. I can see your windows from where I am parked.'

Why was he so close? she wondered.

* * *

Luc sat in his car, stared at the light from the windows of the white-painted cottage a hundred yards away. He had been there for quite some time, wondering, trying to decide what to do. Decide what to do about Dr Kelly Blackman.

Three years ago he had thought he would never fall for another woman. He had been through a painful divorce. Not a difficult divorce, his then wife had been only too pleased to see the back of him. But the divorce had hurt him, he had thought himself genuinely in love, he had tried to make the marriage work. His efforts had been scorned, and it had left him feeling a fool.

So a decision. He would never trust himself to another woman. They just weren't worth the effort. There had been a couple of brief affairs, but both sides had known that they weren't going to last. And Luc had found them ultimately unsatisfying. He had broken both off before anyone had got hurt.

And now, what about Kelly? He had kissed her, she had kissed him back. And both of them had been half happy, half shocked. It had been unplanned, unexpected. But it had been so good. What now?

First, he knew that a mere transitory affair would be no good at all. Not that she would embark upon one, he could sense that. Besides, they had to work together, and to have any kind of affair with a colleague—with someone with whom he would have to work most days—would be the last word in stupidity. No, the sensible thing to do would be to treat Kelly as a colleague and perhaps a friend, but no more.

But…she attracted him. He would put it no stronger than

that. She attracted him. He liked the way she looked, the way she walked, the way she talked. He also was impressed by her medical skills. He didn't *want* just to be friends.

They had only known each other for two days. Nothing had been decided, nothing had been said. They could still finish up just as friends.

He smiled sadly as he started the car engine. Who was he trying to kid?

CHAPTER FOUR

HE WAS going to be here in exactly five minutes? She stood, a quick check in the mirror. Her face would have to remain make-up-less, but, then, it usually did. Time for a quick brush through her hair, make it as presentable as it usually was. Her nightie and dressing-gown were a bit of a problem—both were summer wear, both were light silk, they clung and were even a touch transparent. Well, that was too bad. She wasn't going to get dressed now. Still, a thrill ran through her. What would Luc think—feel—when he saw her like this?

Then the sensible Kelly took over. She ran upstairs, pulled on a pair of sensible white knickers. Just in case.

She was ready. There was a knock at the door. She was excited, a bit nervous. What if he thought that she was inviting him to...? After all, he was French. No, that was a foolish stereotype...and she knew him better than that. She opened the door.

'Kelly, I must apologise for calling so late. Perhaps I had better not come in? I would quite understand if you—'

'Luc, please come in. I invited you because I wanted you to come.'

In his eyes she had seen the flash of appreciation when

he had first seen her. But now as he stepped inside she saw his expression more clearly. There was fatigue, sadness. She felt for him.

She ushered him into her living room, indicated he was to sit in one of the two comfortable armchairs. She sat opposite him, knees firmly pressed together. Then, with a slightly teasing smile, she asked, 'How long have you been waiting outside my house?'

'Perhaps twenty minute,' he confessed. 'I did so want to call but I did not want to be…intrusive?'

'No problem. When I was in medical school there were friends in and out of my room at all hours, day or night, male or female.'

'But that was not so in the army?'

'No,' said Kelly, with a shudder at the very thought. 'Now, what can I get you to drink? I have tea, coffee, wine, spirits. No beer, I'm afraid.'

'What are you having?'

Well, better own up to it. 'Don't laugh. I have a mug of milky cocoa with a shot of brandy in it. Cocoa and brandy makes me sleep and it's better than drugs.'

He managed to keep a straight face. 'It is a drink I have never heard of anyone in France drinking. But I would like to try it. I will not go to sleep at once?'

'You'll stay awake long enough to drive home. Just.'

She went into her kitchen, put the milk on to boil, buttered him another Blackman family scone. She was excited but curious. Where was she going with Luc? Was she heading for another emotional mess? Would it be better if she dropped all contact with Luc as soon as possible? She couldn't go through that emotional turmoil again!

She shrugged. What was to be would be. She took a loaded tray back into the living room.

Obviously he was not the happy, contained man he had been earlier in the day. 'You're thinking of Monsieur Lartigue, aren't you?' she asked gently.

'I am. He had a good life and died happily at home. But he was part of my upbringing. He made me proud to be a soldier.'

Luc looked up then, and his smile was brilliant. 'But now life must move on. I am having supper with a most attractive woman, and if Jean-Paul could see us, then I am sure that he would approve.'

'Quite,' said Kelly. It was a useful word, it meant nothing, it neither approved nor disapproved. But she did like being referred to as a most attractive woman.

'Luc, you just referred to your upbringing. I know so little about you. But you know things about me that I have kept secret from most of the world. I do know that you don't like Englishwomen. That's not much of a beginning for a…for a friendship.' She decided that 'friendship' was the right word. For now.

He laughed. 'It's only one Englishwoman that I really don't like. Or perhaps one Englishwoman and her family. And perhaps they prejudiced me. But now I think I must revise my opinion.'

'Good,' she said. 'Your upbringing?'

'You shall know all that you wish to know. Why don't you come to tea at my home tomorrow afternoon? I have lived there all my life. That will tell you so much about me. And I will answer all your questions.'

'I'd really like that,' she said. But she wondered. Had

there been a flash of apprehension on his face? Was he already regretting the invitation? Whatever, she was going. Then she decided she had imagined it.

She followed him to the door when he was leaving a little later.

'So I will call for you about three tomorrow?' he asked.

'I'd like that.' She opened the door. But he didn't step outside. Instead, he pushed it closed again. Then he took her in his arms, kissed her. His kiss was gentle, like the last one. His arms were loose round her, his kiss not intrusive. She could escape any moment she wanted. But she didn't want. She wanted to stay here for ever, to make more of the way their bodies seemed to fit so well together, more of the way his hands caressed her back, more of the way his tongue had probed so delicately that she…

He broke away from her. 'Until tomorrow, then,' he gasped. 'Kelly, I'm so sorry. I didn't intend to kiss you again. But I did and I'm pleased I did.' And then he was gone.

I feel pleased too, Kelly thought. How strange.

Next morning Kelly took the early bus to Estaville—the nearest large town—to buy another dress. If she was going to visit Luc's home then she wanted to look, well, smart. But she also wanted him to see that she had more than one dress. When she had first come to Riom she had not expected to have much of a social life and had packed accordingly.

And now, instead of just one dress, she had four. And she'd thoroughly enjoyed her shopping expedition. Not that it had anything to do with Luc, but she'd bought new underwear too. And just a little more make-up.

* * *

Luc had said that he would arrive again at three. So at one she started to try on the new dresses she had bought that morning. Things didn't look the same in her own bedroom as they had in the shops in Estaville.

She wasn't sure of the impression she wanted to make on Luc. Perhaps things had happened a little too quickly the day before. But, still, she had spent a fair amount of time and money that morning. She might as well make the most of it.

The lemon dress set off her tan. The line was flattering, it emphasised her slim waist but perhaps the full skirt was a little too long, she ought to take up the hem. The blue dress she had chosen for the softness of the fine cotton fabric, it would be cool on hot summer days. And the low neckline was flattering. The third one was really something. Apparently white, when she turned it shimmered with a variety of rainbow colours that mixed and flowed. She spent some minutes in front of the mirror, pirouetting and admiring herself. Then she sighed, reminding herself that the invitation was for afternoon tea. This was a dress for an evening out in an expensive restaurant. Admit it. She would be overdressed.

So it was the lemon dress. She rummaged in her suitcase, found needle and thread.

At two o'clock she ran a bath, adding some luxurious bath essence. Afterwards she put on her new cream underwear and surveyed herself. The lacy scraps of silk were unlike anything she had chosen before but she liked them. She slipped into the lemon dress. Look good from the inside out.

At twenty to three she sat down to wait. Be calm, be self-possessed. And at five to three she leaped to her feet—she had forgotten the box of scones she had intended to give him yesterday. Of course, he knocked just as she was scrabbling with the wrapping paper.

As ever, he was punctual and he looked as gorgeous as usual. When he smiled at her there was the usual fast thudding of her heart. Would this always happen when she saw him? Would he ever become just another ordinary man? She didn't know—but she didn't think so.

He was wearing another light jacket, this time his shirt was a cream colour. Almost the shade of her... She blushed as she remembered.

'You look ravishing,' he said. 'Please don't take that as part of a Frenchman's normal approach to an attractive woman. I really do mean it. Is that a new dress?'

'It is! How did you guess?'

He pursed his lips. 'Well, when a woman wears a new dress for the first time isn't there a feeling of mixed excitement and apprehension? Does the dress flatter me? Will he like it?'

She felt vulnerable. 'Are you saying that that's how I am feeling now? Does it show?'

'Of course.' He laughed teasingly. 'That and the fact that you told me yesterday that you were wearing the only dress you had brought with you.'

'Luc Laforge! That's not fair! Leading a poor girl on.'

'Sorry,' he said with a grin that said he was not in the least sorry. 'Now, shall we go?'

She took the parcel that she had been holding behind her, handed it to him. 'This time a gift from me. To show that I forgive you. A few of my mother's recipe scones. I meant to give them to you last night but I forgot.'

'These are most welcome,' he said. 'Tonight, for supper. But shall we go?'

She wondered exactly what she was going to.

He walked her round to the passenger side of his car, opened the door for her, made sure that her seat belt was fastened. Then they were off, quickly out of the village.

She liked the Breton countryside. There was the abundance of wild flowers, the odd shapes of the rocks that broke the surface of the fields, the twisted trees that had to fight against the harsh winter winds. It was a mysterious landscape. And there weren't too many people about, that was good too. Luc noticed the way she was staring out of the window, so drove slowly. That was thoughtful of him.

In time they turned off the road, passed a stone gatehouse and drove down a tree-shaded drive. They turned again—and she gasped. There was a tiny fairy-tale castle. Well, a French chateau, really. In the front were gardens bright with red gardenias. A circle of gravel where cars could park. And the chateau itself was in dark cream stone and there were towers, and turrets and pointed windows— it was a dream.

'This is your home? Luc, it is beautiful!'

'It has been in my family for generations. There have been times when I have wanted to give it up, to move into something more modern, more manageable. But I can't. This place doesn't just belong to me, it belongs to the generations to come. Now come and look inside.'

Inside was just as wonderful—but different. A stone-floored hall with a rich red carpet on it. The room wasn't over-grand, it was too small for that. It seemed to be a family home. Certainly there were some oil paintings on the walls but there were also photographs of the surrounding countryside and a couple of framed advertisements for French Railways. Kelly looked round, entranced.

She heard the click of a door opening, turned to see an old lady in black dress with a white pinafore. The lady waved at Luc to come to her. He excused himself, walked over and had a whispered conversation. Kelly carried on looking at the pictures.

After a moment or two Luc led the lady over to Kelly, introduced her as Minette. 'She is my housekeeper. She lives in the gatehouse, has been with my family for years.'

'So pleased to meet you, Minette,' Kelly said.

'Madame,' Minette mumbled, and bobbed a little curtsey.

Kelly was astonished. No one had ever curtseyed to her before.

'Minette is going to make us some tea,' Luc said, and Minette scurried away.

'This house is so lovely,' Kelly said when she had gone. 'You're so lucky to live here.'

'I do like it. Perhaps you would like to look around?'

'I'd like nothing better,' Kelly said, who had been thinking that very thing.

'And later you shall. But first you wanted to know a little more about me. And what I am to show you now is…is perhaps the most important thing in my life. The reason why I am not free to do as I wish.'

He led her down a corridor, quietly opened a door. She was shown into a room at the back of the house, once obviously a conservatory. Now wooden slats shut off most of the sun, there were just a few rays of light across the floor.

Luc held his finger to his lips, led her across the room to a bed. In it was a sleeping child, perhaps six years old. Serious damage had been done to her left leg. Both tibia and fibula had been fractured, an external fixator kept the bones in place. It had been a comminuted fracture, the wounds on her leg were covered with a light dressing. Whatever had happened, this child had suffered.

'This is my daughter, Jenny,' Luc said. 'As you may know from Joe, she's been in an accident.' He looked at Kelly thoughtfully. 'Whatever decisions I make about my life, Jenny must come first. She has suffered more than any child should have to suffer. From now on Jenny's happiness is all-important to me.'

'You mean, if necessary, it must come before your own happiness?'

'Of course.'

'I think that is wonderful.'

The room they were sitting in was impressive. There was a large marble fireplace, antique furniture, a thick oriental-looking carpet on the floor. One wall was completely taken up by bookshelves. But it all looked comfortable, lived-in. Tall windows opened onto a view of lawns and flower-beds. Kelly had stood, admiring the books, while Minette had arranged dishes on the coffee-table. 'Now, tell me about Jenny and her accident,' Kelly said. Luc looked glum. 'That means I have to talk about her mother—my ex-wife.'

'It does,' Kelly confirmed cheerfully. 'Well, don't forget you invited me here to get to know things about you.'

'I suppose you are right.' He stood, walked across the room to a cupboard, and brought back a leather-bound album. 'The French are as obsessed by photographs as the English,' he said. 'I could not bear to throw these away—and it would have been childish to cut out the bits that I would like to forget.'

He put the album on her lap. 'Photographs of my wife, myself and my daughter,' he said. 'They show something of our life together.'

'No wedding photographs?' Kelly asked, after leafing through a few pages.

'I burned all the photographs of our wedding that I had.'

Kelly winced at the bitterness in his tone.

They were interesting photographs, mostly of Jenny growing up, from a baby to a child of about four years old.

'I see all the captions are in English,' Kelly commented.

'Jenny is bilingual—and very good in both languages. But Merryl could not be bothered to learn French. As she pointed out, I spoke good English—what was the point?'

Kelly decided not to comment. It wasn't her place to judge.

She was fascinated by the pictures of Merryl, who was just the opposite of herself. Kelly was glad about that. Merryl was blonde, thin, classically good looking, and in the photographs always well dressed.

'Your ex-wife was very beautiful,' Kelly ventured.

'There is an English saying that I like. "Beauty is only skin deep."'

Kelly was rather surprised at that. She had not thought that Luc was a man who could express himself so…well, so forcibly. He must have been hurt very deeply by this woman.

She looked through further, noting that there were fewer and fewer pictures with Luc in them. But Merryl was usually there, smiling, looking gorgeous. Then Kelly noticed something else. In all the pictures Merryl was carefully posed. There were none of the usual happy family snaps, taken at just the wrong embarrassing moment. 'Was your wife a model?' she asked.

'How did you know that?'

'It's the way that she always looks elegant. As if she was used to a camera.'

Luc sighed. 'Yes, she was a model. She didn't need to be, she came from a rich family. A charming girl, much fun to be with, but she… Whatever she wanted she had to have. We had a lightning courtship while I was on a course in London. I brought her here before we were married, she said she loved the place. After the first winter she changed her mind. She needed to be in London with her family and friends. Especially her male friends.'

'Didn't she want to be with Jenny?'

'Jenny was a fashion accessory. Otherwise Merryl spoiled her or ignored her.'

Luc stood, walked over to the window, stared out as she had done. Kelly realised what he was doing. He did not want her to see his face. This was painful for him.

'I tried as hard as I could to please Merryl but there was no pleasing her for long. So we got divorced. I kept Jenny. Merryl had visiting rights, of course, but a child would only upset Merryl's complicated social life. Jenny and I were happy here together. We had a nurse as a nanny, Edith Lachalle, and she too was devoted to Jenny. Then two or three months ago Edith fell pregnant and there were problems. She became hypertensive and, in fact, I ordered her to stop work. I told Merryl, who said that she would take Jenny for a few days until I organised another nanny. I wasn't very happy about it but…

'Merryl came here in her new sports car, picked up Jenny. On her way back to the ferry she stopped for lunch, had too much to drink and crashed the car. Jenny—well, you have seen the state she is in. As ever, Merryl had nothing but a few scratches. But Jenny could have been killed! So now my lawyers are having her assessed as an unfit parent. Merryl doesn't seem too bothered about it.'

'Perhaps she thought that Jenny was getting as beautiful as her,' Kelly said slyly. 'She didn't want the competition.'

Luc turned and laughed. 'Dr Blackman, you flatter like a Frenchman. I think that my daughter is beautiful but—yes, Minette?'

Somehow, silently Minette had entered the room and obviously needed to talk to Luc. Kelly looked down at the albums in front of her, for the moment pretended to be engrossed.

There was a whispered conversation and then Luc turned to Kelly. He looked upset. 'There is a problem,' he said. 'I am not on call but I have to go out—it is a police matter, they need me to examine someone as a matter of urgency. I have agreed to do this kind of work, but usually I am only called out once or twice a year. Why today and now?'

'Because that is the way that emergency work comes in,' Kelly said cheerfully.

'Hortense, a young niece of Minette's, comes in quite often and sits with Jenny. But she isn't here now. I expected to be here myself. So now, when she wakes, I must ask Minette to—'

'Could I sit with Jenny?' Kelly asked. 'Would that help?'

'It would help a lot. But why should you want to do that?'

'In a few days I'm going to be working for you. Perhaps

I just want to please the boss.' She grinned, to show it was a joke. 'Luc, you know it makes sense.'

'Right. I accept. I'll tell Minette, she will introduce you to Jenny when she wakes up. Kelly, I think I'm really going to enjoy working with you.'

Only working? Kelly thought.

'It hurts sometimes and sometimes it itches and I don't like it,' Jenny said. 'And I can't get out and walk in the garden and run or swim and it's just not fair.'

Kelly saw the little face start to crumple and knew that she had to find something to say, some way to stop the threatened tears. 'I've got an idea,' she said. Then she wondered quite what it was.

She was somebody, something new to Jenny. This was an advantage. Jenny was obviously usually an active child and was not taking well to being confined to bed. She was bored. Kelly had quickly realised that her main job was to keep Jenny entertained, stop her from fretting, get her interested in something. What?

Then she thought of the slightly older girls she had helped in the car crash. They had written her a letter. That was an idea.

'How long were you in hospital, Jenny?' she asked.

'I was in for five days. I didn't like it there but the nurses were nice to me. They held my hand when it hurt and I was crying.'

'Well, I can hold your hand if you like but I don't think it will hurt any more.' She took hold of Jenny's hand. 'Here, and you're not even crying. Were there any nurses that you specially remember?'

'There was Helene and there was Françoise. They gave me a card when I left. That was nice.'

'Would you like to write them a letter saying thank you for looking after you? And perhaps do a drawing of something for them?'

Kelly smiled at Jenny, hoping that she could not see that she had her fingers crossed behind her.

Jenny frowned as she thought. 'I think that would be nice,' she said. 'I've got coloured pencils and there's some paper for drawing over there. Will you help me?'

'Certainly. I'll help. But you must remember that this is a letter and a drawing from you, because you're special. Now, where did you say the paper was kept?'

Kelly enjoyed her stay with Jenny. Of course she had done some paediatric work when she had first studied, but since then had treated few children. But she remembered her own rather lonely childhood and that helped.

And time seemed to pass quickly. Her ideas intrigued Jenny. Once or twice Minette came in, just to make sure that all was well. But otherwise Jenny and Kelly played together.

It was about two hours before Luc returned. He came into Jenny's room, carrying a glass of milk for Jenny, a glass of fruit juice for her.

'Daddy, Daddy!' Jenny opened her arms as best she could. Luc leaned over and gave her a gentle hug, a kiss, and then sat on the side of the bed. 'How are you feeling, little girl?'

'I've written a letter! And Auntie Kelly says you will send it to the nurses in the hospital where I was 'cos they will want to know how I am.'

'I'm sure they will.' Luc studied the sheet of paper that

Jenny had passed him. 'This is a very good letter. And a good drawing too!'

'That's me in bed with the fix—fix thing on my leg,' Jenny said importantly. 'Daddy, can Auntie Kelly come to stay with us?'

'I'm afraid not, darling. She has her own home.'

'Sometimes she could come and hold me when I cry in the night. Like you do. And then you could get more sleep.'

'You're going to stop crying in the night soon because you are getting better. Now, drink your milk. It makes bones mend.'

This was a side of Luc that Kelly hadn't seen before. He was tender. The love he had for his daughter was so obvious when he stroked her hair, when he held the glass to her mouth, when he kissed her gently on the cheek.

I wish I had someone who could love me like that, Kelly thought to herself. Then she blanched. What was she thinking?

CHAPTER FIVE

KELLY blinked. 'Go out for dinner? On Saturday night? I haven't eaten out once since I arrived in France. Just an occasional coffee in the town-centre café in the morning. But that's been all.'

'Because you did not want to mix with people?' Luc guessed.

'Something like that. I liked cooking for myself. I got used to my own company.'

'I wish to take you to dinner. Perhaps as a small thank you for looking after Jenny so well this afternoon. Nothing too flashy, a small *auberge* I know that specialises in local food. And I promise that if you are not happy with the meal I will never ask you out again.' He shook his head. 'But I have every confidence in Malouf's cooking.'

She remained silent a moment. Then, in a flat voice, 'But I don't go out much among people. I've been happy in my own little world. It's been all right you coming to see me in the cottage, or me coming to your house. But this is different.'

She blinked as she thought of the enormity of it. 'This is a date!'

He winced. 'Having a date is what American teenagers do. I don't like the word. We are slightly more mature, we are having a…a…'

'An assignation?' she suggested with a grin. 'Never mind what we call it. I would like to go to dinner with you.'

'Good.' He smiled at her and she felt excited and reckless and certain that she had made the right decision. But then she wondered. Still—it was now too late.

Luc had said he was taking her to a small *auberge*. She was beginning to wonder just what his idea of a small *auberge* might be. This was one reason why she decided to bathe and change her dress.

So, more of the new-bought underwear. Lilac this time. Then the shot silk dress. A last check that her make-up was in place, her hair carefully arranged. Yes, all was well. She checked her watch. Ten minutes before she had said she would meet him. She could barely suppress her excitement about spending more time with Luc.

Yet only four short days ago she had never met him. She had been more or less content in her life, used to it and well aware that things had been much worse. One thing had been certain. After Gary she was not interested in men.

Then she had met Luc. She had liked him, she had been kissed by him, had kissed him back. What had got into her? Luc was a man, an attractive man, and he obviously found her attractive. He was a danger to her! If she gave way, if she found herself falling for him, she knew she would be in trouble.

Not all men were like Gary, a little voice told her. Well, that might be true. But many of them were.

* * *

She was glad that she had made some kind of effort. Apart from anything else, Luc had always been perfectly dressed when he had called on her. And he was tonight. A darker suit, white shirt again and a silk tie in a burgundy colour.

He seemed to find the same thing to admire in her dress. Before she knew what he was doing, he had taken her two hands in his, swung her round so he could see her in the light of the low sun. 'Kelly, tonight you look exquisite. You will be the most beautiful woman in the auberge.'

'What did you tell me before about French men being flatterers?' she teased.

He shook his head sadly. 'The trouble with being a Frenchman is that no woman believes him, even when he is telling the truth. Once again, you look exquisite.'

'I may look exquisite but I'm feeling hungry,' she told him.

He shook his head in mock horror. 'Beauty must come before food. But…let us go.'

Kelly had half expected that they would go to one of the larger towns or villages along the coast. But instead they drove inland a little, following the bank of a river. Eventually they stopped at a riverside village, little more than a hamlet.

Luc parked in the central square. There were quite a few other cars there, but no obvious tourists to be seen. Luc saw her looking around, guessed what she was thinking. 'The patrons of this *auberge* don't talk about the place,' he said. 'It is a secret we wish to keep to ourselves.'

'Doesn't this Malouf want to advertise? To make money?'

Luc shook his head. 'All he wants to do is cook for those who appreciate good food. His wife runs the *auberge*. All she wants to do is see her guests enjoying their meal, appreciating the food. They are a happy couple. Now we have to walk a little way.'

He led her through the narrow streets until they reached the banks of the river. There was a long narrow building, shaded by trees. They entered and were instantly greeted by a tiny bubbling lady in a black dress. 'Dr Laforge! So good to see you again. And your charming companion?'

'Madame Malouf, good to see you too. This is Dr Blackman, we are to work together for a while.'

'Welcome to L'Auberge de la Rivière, Dr Blackman. May I say that your dress is most chic.'

'Thank you,' said Kelly, and felt rather pleased.

'I have a table ready for you,' Madame Malouf said. 'I have your bottle of wine ready chilled.' She turned and led the two through a wide opening into… 'Goodness! this is a beautiful room,' Kelly gasped.

In fact, it wasn't a room. It was a terrace, with a cane ceiling to protect the clients from the sun. One side was completely open and below it she could see and hear the river. Tables were scattered around, not too close together. Most were occupied and there was the hum of quiet conversation, But most people seemed to be occupied with eating.

'We believe fine food should be eaten in fine surroundings,' Madame Malouf said proudly.

She led them to what Kelly had to think must be the best table. It was in a corner, overlooking the river. A blue and white checked tablecloth, the sparkle of glasses and the shine of silver cutlery.

Madame Malouf saw that they were seated, took a bottle from a silver ice bucket and showed the label to Luc. 'Your favourite,' she said.

'My favourite. Madame Malouf, what shall I do when it has all been drunk?'

'We will always find a bottle for you. Shall I open it?'

'Please do.'

With bewildering speed Madame had produced a cork-screw from somewhere about her person, had pulled the cork and reconcealed the corkscrew before Kelly could quite grasp what was happening. Then half an inch of wine was poured into Luc's glass.

He lifted the glass by its stem, smelled the wine and then took a sip. 'Yes,' he said after a moment's reflection. 'Madame, your cellar is as wonderful as ever.'

Madame looked gratified. She half filled Kelly's glass, did the same to Luc's. 'Now, I leave you for a while. The menu.' And she was gone.

Luc pushed Kelly's glass of white wine towards her. 'I hope you like this. It's from a small vineyard on the Loire. It's a very light wine, very delicate, it goes well with the cooking here.'

As she had seen Luc do, Kelly smelled then sipped the wine. Yes, she could get to like this. It was delicate. At first there didn't seem to be too much taste. But as she held it in her mouth the taste seemed to grow.

'Do you like it?' Luc's voice was anxious.

'I love it. It seems to get better as you drink it. It's like a…'

Then she froze. What on earth had made her say something like that? But she hadn't said it yet, it was a foolish idea, if she spoke she would only embarrass Luc and be embarrassed herself.

'It's like a…?' Luc questioned.

She could tell from his teasing tone that he knew she

had started something she did not now want to finish. What could she say? Was it like a flower or a spring morning or the touch of a baby's skin? None of those. Well, brazen it out. 'I was going to say that it was like a kiss,' she said.

He looked at her. Took another sip of wine. 'Yes,' he said thoughtfully, 'I see what you mean. The question now must be—would you rather drink this wine or be kissed?'

'I think I'd rather look at the menu,' she said.

He smiled, said nothing, and passed a menu over to her.

It was no good. Her French was excellent, she could understand what was on offer. But the words just whirled in front of her. Too many decisions! She couldn't make up her mind. She closed the menu, pushed it across to Luc. 'You must understand that for the past six months I've been living on my own. I've existed on simple stuff, sand-wiches and fruit and salad. My idea of a mad night's cook-ing has been making a vegetable soup. Choosing anything from this menu is beyond me.'

'There's no problem. If you like, I will order for both of us.' He smiled. 'And since whenever you order here, you always wish you had ordered what your companion ordered—I will order the same for us both.'

'That will simplify things.'

Luc was now deep in conversation with Madame. There was much pointing at the menu, frowning, pursing the lips, occasionally nodding in agreement. This choice was obvi-ously a serious matter. But eventually it was done. Madame smiled and swept away.

Luc reached over, stroked the back of her hand. It was something he had done before, a gentle, non-threatening caress that she rather liked. 'Do you like it here?' he asked. 'I promised that we could go home if you felt unsettled.'

'I don't want to go home and I do like it here. I like Madame. It's just all so different from what I've been used to.'

'Just take a step at a time,' he advised. 'You will feel even better after the meal. Ah, course one.'

Course one was soup. A plate with a rounded soup bowl on it, a lid on the bowl. To one side a small dish of croutons. The waiter deferentially placed the bowl in front of her and took off the lid. Kelly leaned forward, smelled. It was wonderful! Fishy, but not too much so. Then she looked. A smooth creamy soup coloured a glorious yellow. Yellow soup? She looked at Luc enquiringly.

'Every course here will have been largely sourced locally,' he said. 'This is mussel soup with saffron. Mussels from this river estuary. Try it.'

She did. Once again, as with the wine, the first effect was mild—but the taste developed. 'I'm going to enjoy this,' she told him. And she did.

It was an obvious policy of the *auberge* that the courses did not follow each other too quickly. In between there was time to talk, to reflect on what had just been eaten. Or to talk about other things.

'How often do you come here?' she asked him.

He shrugged. 'Perhaps once a fortnight. I don't like to come too often—I want every visit to be an occasion. Something that I will remember. I have eaten here on my own. The food, of course, is always superb—but I believe that a good meal is greatly improved by good company.

Your company makes this meal far far more enjoyable than if I were here on my own.'

'Another French compliment!'

'But what I said is true!'

'Luc, I believe you. It's just that the last few months I've not shared a meal with anyone. Never wanted to either. I've been perfectly…not happy on my own but it was what I wanted. This is all very different.'

'Another course,' he said.

It was wonderful again. On one small plate there was a selection of tiny vegetables—broccoli, asparagus, spring onions, shining with the hot butter that had been dribbled on them. On a larger plate was chicken in a thick sauce—creamed potatoes to one side. And the smell!

'Cider chicken,' Luc said. 'Local free-range chicken, local cider made from local apples. But you can still drink the wine with the chicken. It will not clash with the cider.'

'Right,' said Kelly.

Another course, not finished quickly but slowly and appreciatively. And when the plates had been removed there was more time to sit and talk.

'Are you losing your fear now?' Luc asked. 'Do you feel comfortable, with me and with the people around you?'

Not an easy question to answer. 'I feel there are two Kellys,' she told him. 'Right now, the Kelly you see is happy with your company and enjoying herself and looking forward to the next three months. But there's another Kelly looking over her shoulder, who is scared and certain that something soon will go wrong.'

'Perhaps that is a Kelly we can do without. In time she will disappear.'

'Perhaps. Now, that's a smell I can recognise before it gets to the table. That's the smell of pastry. Every member of the Blackman family recognises that.'

The plates were put in front of them. 'Our dessert. Apple galette with cream,' said Luc.

'Now, this is a dessert to die for.'

There was coffee to finish and a tiny glass each of Calvados—the fiery Breton spirit made of apples. Then an enthusiastic goodbye from Madame and a request that they visit her more often. A quick glimpse of the kitchen and a shouted greeting to a steam-enshrouded Malouf, who smiled but was too busy to leave his work.

'You didn't need to leave, then?' Luc joked amiably as they walked back to the car.

'You knew I wouldn't. Luc, that was the most enjoyable evening I've spent in probably years. Can we go back some time? And can I treat you next time?'

'If you really wish to. But I am happy to escort you. Now, shall I take you home?'

To her amazement she discovered that she didn't want to go straight back to her cottage. She was happy out with Luc. She wanted things to stay that way.

She looked upwards, pointed to the sky. 'The stars are so clear. And look at the size of that moon. It's bright enough to read by.'

He smiled. 'You wish to read by moonlight?'

'No. I want to walk. My shoes are reasonable enough. Just for half an hour I'd like to walk in the moonlight.'

'Then we will drive back to the sea and walk along the promenade at Riom. At this time of night there will be no other people there.'

'That is a lovely idea.'

Fifteen minutes later they were standing on the promenade. A stone path that led from the village centre along the seafront to an old lighthouse on a promontory. There were a couple of bistros open in the village but only a handful of customers. People in this area went to bed early. The promenade was deserted. After they had walked a couple of hundred metres they were away from all sight or sound of humanity.

'Now, that is beautiful,' Kelly said. The moon had risen a little since they had left the *auberge* and seemed to shine even brighter. From it, a line of silver fire seemed to cross the dark blue ocean, to shatter into fragments where the waves beat quietly on the sand.

'It is indeed,' he said.

'And the air is not too hot, not too cool, there's a slight wind blowing towards us and it carries the scent of the sea. What could be more wonderful?'

'If I tell you, you'll say I'm being a typical Frenchman again.'

'I promise not to.'

'Then I'd say it would be more wonderful if I had the hand of a beautiful woman to hold.'

She thought about that. 'You can make do with this one if you like.'

He took her hand, for a moment raised it to his lips and kissed it. 'This is more than making do,' he said.

They walked on in silence for a while. She liked having him hold her hand. From time to time he squeezed her fingers, or ran one of his fingers across the palm of her hand. 'When I was very young,' she told him, 'I knew nothing about boys, or only what other girls told me. And the bigger girls said that if a boy did that to you—you know, stroke the palm of your hand—then it meant that he wanted to…' She decided to say no more.

'That he wanted to what?' Luc teased.

'You know very well,' she said primly. 'That he wanted to kiss you. And let me say, right now, that is not an invitation.'

'Now, that is a pity.'

Eventually they reached the end of the promenade. There were steps leading down to the beach. Kelly looked at the strip of clean sand, at the tiny waves crisping on the edge of the beach.

'I want to paddle,' she said.

'You want to what?'

'I want to paddle. I'm feeling in the mood for doing… for doing different things.'

'Then if that is what you want, I shall take off my shoes ands socks, roll up my trousers and paddle with you.'

'You don't have to,' she said doubtfully.

'Perhaps I want to. Now, let me help you down these steps. In the dark they could be slippery.' He jumped down and then turned and reached out to her. Holding his two hands, she stepped downwards till she was on the beach with him. But he hadn't let go. And they were standing not six inches apart.

He kissed her. Only their hands and their lips were touching but for the moment she thought that that was enough. But it was so nice. His lips were warm, inviting. It was a tender kiss, but one she thought that had the promise of more. Perhaps if she released his hand he might…

He thought that too. But when he did let go of her, she

stepped back. 'That was very pleasant but for the moment I think it is enough,' she said.

She felt the anguish in his voice. 'Enough, Kelly? It wasn't enough for me.'

'Then shall we say enough for now. Now, are we going to paddle or not?'

She kicked off her shoes. He balanced on one foot and took off shoes and socks, rolled up his trouser legs. 'If any of my patients see me doing this,' he said, 'I'll never dare send in a bill again.'

'Learn to live dangerously. Now, come on!' Hand in hand they ran down to the sea edge.

She felt so good walking along in the ankle-deep water, the occasional little wave splashing over her calves. The water was refreshing. She felt it brought life to her.

'I've not done anything as silly as this in years,' she said, 'and I'm thoroughly enjoying it. I feel it's doing me good. Thank you for bringing me here, Luc.'

She leaned towards him for the quickest of kisses. On the cheek.

'I think it was largely your idea,' he said mildly. 'But I am enjoying myself. Have you ever come down here to swim, Kelly? In the daytime, of course?'

'No. Never.' Now her mood had altered. She could paddle in the sea in the dark, when no one could see her. But the idea of coming down here when there were crowds on the beach, of showing her half-naked body to anyone who might be passing—that would be intolerable.

He seemed to understand her qualms. 'Perhaps you'll get used to it in time. No need to hurry. Now, the car's up there. I think it's time we climbed back to the promenade.'

'Don't forget to roll your trousers back down,' she warned him.

It was going to happen, she knew it, and she was even looking forward to it. They stopped in the shadow of the promenade and he put his arms round her. No need for false modesty now. This was what she wanted, and they both knew it. He pulled her to him. This was not the man who had gently touched her lips with his—this was a man who wanted, needed her in every possible way. In an almost detached fashion she was aware of his excitement, of the beating of his heart, of his arousal against her thigh.

He kissed her. There was no past, no future, the world dissolved so that there was only the now. He kissed her and she kissed him back, opening her lips to the urgent pressure of his tongue, giving him a first tentative entrance to her body. Her hands clutched at his head, her body reacted to his, she knew he could feel the softness of her breasts as she pressed closer to him, feel the hardness of her nipples. She heard him groan with pleasure.

Her body told her. This could only lead to one thing, something now desperately needed by both of them. They could drive back to his house, they could…

The only alternative was to stop now. But perhaps just a few more minutes of bliss and then they could… No. It would only make things harder. If that were possible.

It was the hardest thing she had ever done. She took her arms from round him, placed her hands on his shoulders and gently pushed him away.

He was Luc, always a gentleman. He stepped back as she wanted him to, but his reluctance was obvious. 'Kelly, *chérie*, what is the matter? I did not wish to…I thought that you…'

Her voice was quavering but she knew this had to be said. 'If you kiss me much more as you are doing, you know where it will lead.'

'It will lead only to where you want to go.'

Sadly, she shook her head. 'I know it will lead to where I want to go. Let's say it. My body tells me I want, I need to go to bed with you. But my brain says—what then? If we make love then all I can see in my future is… Luc, I just can't get over the chaos and misery that Gary left me in. I don't know what I want! Luc, I desperately want to…and I'm sorry if you feel I led you on. I didn't intend to.'

He took her hand, raised it to his lips and kissed it. His voice shook as he said, 'I won't say it doesn't matter because that would be a lie. But at times we are all disturbed. Gary is now just a ghost in your past, in time he will disappear. There is a ghost in my past too, like yours, the ghost of a past love affair. But that will disappear too. Now I will walk you quietly back to the car and then I will drive you home. It has been a full day, you must be exhausted.'

'It has been a wonderful day, Luc. You have made it that way. But I would like to go home now. Will we…go out again together?'

'I can think of nothing better.'

It was a good thing for Kelly to hear. But she could detect the sadness in his voice. She had offered him something he wanted—and then withdrawn the offer. And now she felt guilty.

The visit to L'Auberge de la Rivière had been one of the most wonderful experiences of Kelly's life. She had always been a guarded person, careful with her emotions. That was why the end of her affair with Gary had been so destructive. She had let her guard down, had offered herself unconditionally. And been rejected. But a few minutes in Luc's arms had meant more to her than her entire time with Gary. Which was why she had had to stop. She had been too frightened to carry on.

And Luc had been so good about it! He had driven her home, talking about nothing much in particular, ignoring her monosyllabic answers. She realised that he wanted her to know that he was not angry with her. They were civilised people. But she also knew how much her refusal had cost him. He tried to make his voice cheerful, the subjects he talked about were ordinary, simple things. But she could detect the hurt underneath. He had reached out to her, expecting to be welcomed, and she had rejected him. But what else could she have done?

CHAPTER SIX

To HER surprise she slept well that night. As Luc had driven her home she had wondered if she ought to invite him in, just for a nightcap, of course. Then she'd decided that it would be foolish, as well as being unlikely. They would never stop short at a nightcap.

She had realised that she'd had a glimpse of possible—just possible—happiness. But going further with Luc would be premature. There were three months of work with him to come, she would see what happened then.

In the event, she hadn't had to decide whether or not to invite him in. He'd left the car engine running as he'd escorted her to her front door, shaken her hand and said, 'That was a wonderful evening.' And then he'd left.

Kelly nodded to herself. Luc knew exactly what she wanted. Just a little time.

Next morning she turned on her radio, found a French pop station. She recognised the song, it was popular in England at the moment so cheerfully she sang along with it… 'I love you and you love me, what's our future, we will see…' It was so long since she had sung to herself. She must be changing.

It happened while she was in the little kitchen. She was singing, wondering when she would see Luc again.

Then suddenly her world exploded. There was the scream of metal on metal, the splintering of breaking glass, the crash of falling masonry. She opened her mouth to scream, it filled with dust. Something smashed into her chest, she was thrown backwards and her head hit the stone floor.

There was time for just one thought. This was France, not the Middle East.

She didn't think she was concussed, didn't even fully lose consciousness. For a while she just lay there, trying to make sense of what had happened. She tried to peer through the brick dust. What was the front of a lorry doing in her living room?

Just for a moment there was a feeling of utter desolation. This cottage had been a haven for her. She had been through all this before, seen too many half-destroyed buildings. Rooms with smashed pictures, ornaments, holding memories of once peaceful lives. Not again!

Then, painfully, she rolled over, climbed up onto her knees. No, not again. She would not go down the route again. Whatever had just happened, now she could cope. This was an accident. Nothing more.

She managed to push herself onto her feet, stagger to the front door. The street was filling with people, she heard the mutter of dismay as they saw her. Her next-door neighbour came over, threw a blanket round her, slipped an arm round her waist. 'Come, you must sit. Is there anyone still in the house?'

Kelly shook her head, coughed, and then said, 'I was on my own.' She looked back at her cottage. The cab of a large lorry was buried deep in the end wall. It was obvious what had happened. The lorry's brakes must have failed as it had negotiated the bend at the bottom of the steep hill leading down into the village. And her cottage had been in the way.

She was a doctor, she was conscious and capable. Just. 'Where is the driver of the lorry? Has he been injured? Is anyone injured?'

'The lorry driver is shocked but otherwise fine. I will tell him that you are not badly injured, he is worried. Now, you will come into my house and rest.'

She was taken into the neighbour's house, made to lie on a couch and another blanket wrapped round her. Somehow, she did rest. She knew she was not badly injured, there was pain but not too much. She thought she'd just close her eyes for a moment, there didn't seem to be much that she could do. Just close her eyes for a moment.

When she opened her eyes there was Luc looking down at her. She had just time to register how worried he looked, remembered how easily his feelings could show on his face. In fact, there was more than worry. There was… He saw that she was awake, and his expression turned to that of the concerned doctor.

'I was at home, your neighbour phoned me and I came at once,' he said. 'Kelly how do you feel?'

She decided that she must be still shocked a little, she said what she felt without thinking. 'I'm glad to see you,' she said, 'so glad.'

'I'm glad to see you're all right. Now, I'll make a quick examination and then we'll get you off to hospital for a thorough check.'

'No need for hospital! Luc, I'm not too badly hurt.

Tomorrow I'll be fine. I just don't know what to do about the cottage.'

'Don't worry about that. I've been in touch with the *mairie*, they'll organise everything very efficiently. But we need to get you seen to.'

And suddenly the doctor disappeared for a moment and the man appeared. 'Kelly when I heard… No one knew how badly you might have been hurt… You could have been dead… And I thought that if you were dead I…'

Then the doctor reappeared. 'Just tell me where it hurts most and I'll decide if you need to go to hospital or not.'

'It hurts that you won't trust my professional judgement!'

'A doctor who treats herself has a fool for a patient,' he quoted. 'Now, let me look at you.'

He examined her just enough to decide that there was no chance of her getting worse. Then he told her to rest, said he was going to see how things were progressing outside.

He was back ten minutes later. 'All organised. You're not going to hospital, you're coming home with me. I've phoned Minette, she's preparing a bedroom for you.'

'But what about my things? For a start, I need clothes.'

'We can come back for them some other time. The *mairie* has arranged emergency building work, by this afternoon most of the cottage will be safe to enter.'

'But where am I to live?'

'For the moment I would like it if you would live with me. That is, as my guest in my house.'

'Luc, that's so good of you. But—'

'There are definite buts. May I suggest that we leave them until you feel better.'

Kelly thought. 'There's not much I can say, is there?'

'Nothing at all,' Luc said.

Luc was a doctor. He was accustomed to emergencies, knew how it was necessary to keep calm, that personal feelings were a trap. He glanced at the figure by his side, huddled in a blanket. All he had heard was that there had been an accident, Kelly was inside a badly damaged building, no one had known how badly she might have been injured. Or even if she was alive or not. When he had heard this Luc's world had turned upside down. She couldn't be dead, he'd only just met her, and since then his life had been full of more hope than he'd had for months. Now he knew she was alive, she was coming to stay with him. Now he had some idea of what his life would be like if she wasn't around to share it. He would have to be extra-careful not to lose her. Not to push her too far or too fast.

Kelly's room in Luc's home was on the ground floor, next door to Jenny's room and vastly more luxurious than the cottage had been. There her bedroom had been tiny, with sloping walls and a chest of drawers and wardrobe that both rocked when she stood on the wrong floorboard. The bathroom had been along the corridor. Her new room was different. The walls were panelled, the furniture antique, the bed a four-poster with a very modern mattress. And her bathroom was majestic in marble and brass. There were two vases of fresh flowers. Kelly shook her head. If she couldn't be happy in this room then there was no hope for her.

But…before she could think about being happy in the future, there was the present to consider. She was covered in dust, standing in filthy clothes with nothing to change into. There was a rough dressing on her head, she felt sticky and altogether unpleasant. And what was Luc saying? This was something she had not considered.

'I need to examine you properly, Kelly. Then you need a bath and to go to bed for a while. I'll arrange for you to visit the cottage later.'

'Luc, I'm fine, there is no need to examine me. I'm a doctor, I should know. A bath certainly, but otherwise…'

'Dr Blackman, if a patient came to you, having suffered what you have suffered, would you let them go without an examination?'

A pause. 'No,' she muttered.

'Are you embarrassed at the prospect of being examined by a man?'

She had to be honest, tell him what they both knew to be true. 'I am embarrassed at the prospect of being examined by you.'

He nodded. 'I understand. And I am embarrassed at having to put you through this. But it has to be done!'

She had been examined, treated by men before, there was no problem to that. And Luc was the perfect, gentle doctor. There was no sign that he was aware that she was a woman, he was a man. In fact, when he examined the great bruise on her chest, it was she who felt the surge of excitement as he touched her breast. Only when he had finished did she detect the gleam of joint disappointment and delight in his eyes.

'Have a bath now,' he said, 'then go to bed. You were

quite right, there's nothing seriously wrong with you. But you've been shocked, you need the rest. And tomorrow you take things very easy indeed.'

Then he frowned. 'I've put one of my dressing-gowns on the bed for you. This evening we'll find you some clothes that might do for now.' And he was gone.

Clothes? Kelly wondered. Surely he wasn't going to borrow from Minette?

The bath was sheer delight. She shampooed her hair, taking care with the great lump she felt on the back of her head. Then she wrapped herself in a towel, put on his dressing-gown and slid into bed.

She liked the dressing-gown. It was black silk, Chinese in style and smelled, very vaguely, of his cologne.

When he came back he was carrying a tray with a bowl of soup, rolls, a plate of fruit and coffee. 'Minette thinks that you might need something to keep up your strength. So eat what you can of this before you sleep. Now, I must go, I have to work.'

He came to her bedside, leaned over and kissed her—on the forehead. 'I am so glad that you're not badly hurt,' he said. And he was gone.

Kelly slept. She awoke early in the evening, to find pain-killers and a glass of water by her bedside. She felt much better. Then she slept again. There was no cause for worry, sleep was the best possible remedy for shock. The second time she woke there was Luc by her bedside. 'How do you feel, Kelly?'

'Infinitely better. I want to get up and there are things I have to decide.'

'In a moment.' He smiled at her. 'I feel no shame in doing this to you since I know you would do exactly the same to me. A quick check first. Pulse, BP and heart.'

'Whatever,' she sighed. He was, of course, quite right.

When he had finished she said, 'There are things we have to sort out. First of all, I feel at a disadvantage lying here in your dressing-gown while you're fully dressed. Could we go back to the cottage and—?'

He held up his hand. 'We can't get into the cottage before six tomorrow evening but after that we can take what you wish. Your car is there, quite unharmed. I've phoned Joe Cameron, explained things to him, put him in touch with the *mairie*. He has an advocate here who will deal with the legal matters.'

'That's good of you, Luc—going to all this trouble for me. But what about clothes till then?'

He frowned again but then said, 'There's no shortage of clothes. Come with me.'

He took her upstairs, showed her into a large bedroom. Kelly blinked. She had never been in a bedroom that had so obviously been decorated with no thought given to cost. The cream carpet was thick, the brocaded curtains were swagged and held back by gold cords, the chandelier was immense. There was a double bed on a raised platform, a dressing-table with enough lights to illuminate the entire house. One wall was built-in wardrobes.

Kelly didn't like it. 'Is this your bedroom?' she asked.

'No. It was my wife's bedroom. Designed for her by one of her designer friends. I haven't slept in it since she left.'

He opened the door of one of the wardrobes. 'All these

clothes are no longer needed.' Once again Kelly felt the force of Luc's bitterness. He went on, 'I was told to send these to charity—or get rid of them in any way I wished. So far I have not bothered. But all of them are freshly washed or newly cleaned. Take what you wish.'

'I'm not sure I'm happy about wearing your ex-wife's clothes, Luc.'

He shrugged. 'I understand that.' Then he smiled. 'But you don't mind wearing my dressing-gown?'

'No. I really like it.' Then she blushed and said, 'If you're sure she wouldn't mind, I would like to borrow something.'

'Please do. She will never wear any of them again.'

In fact, Kelly was bemused by what she saw. She would have liked to have spent an hour sorting through the contents of the wardrobe. Merryl might have no taste in bedroom furniture, but her clothes were…

'Trousers, two shirts and a sweater, a tracksuit,' she said after five minutes. 'And after I've worn them I insist that I have them cleaned and returned.'

'As you wish. Now, will you get dressed and we will have dinner together?'

'I've just had a call from the *mairie* and a call from a builder,' he told her an hour later. 'The cottage will be rebuilt, as good as new in a fortnight. You may move back in then. Until then I would like you to stay with me.'

'Is that a good idea?'

He knew what she was talking about. 'Perhaps not. Having the two of us together in the same building might be…hazardous.'

That's a good way of putting it, Kelly thought. The very presence of Luc was exciting her. But she merely said, 'So what do we do?'

He sighed. 'Kelly, there is something growing between us. I think something wonderful. But you are frightened of it—and so am I.'

She nodded, sadly. 'That is true.'

'So I propose that…that while you are here as my guest, while you are still perhaps suffering from shock, that we agree that…that we take things no further. We will stay as friends.' Then, in a totally different voice, he added, 'But that is just for now!'

'I agree,' Kelly said after a moment's thought. And she was aware of a tiny touch of disappointment. But she went on, 'I think we can cope. But if I stay here I will have to—'

'I hope you are not going to insult me by talking about money!'

'No. But I would like to help in some way. I thought I might spend time with Jenny when you are not here. She must get bored.'

'That is a great idea,' he said.

'I'll start first thing tomorrow morning.'

It was odd. Kelly found it easier to get on with a child than she did with adults.

'Medicines first and then a wash. Afterwards we'll have breakfast together and then…what would you like to do then?'

'Don't know. I want to go out to walk round the garden but I can't.' Like a lot of invalids, Jenny was not at her best when she first woke up.

'We'll see what we can arrange.' Kelly thought for a minute. 'Do you like birds?'

'Birds?' That was obviously a strange question.

'Yes, birds. In the garden. You must have heard them singing this morning.'

'They sing every morning, just as it gets light,' Jenny said gloomily. 'They wake me up when my leg hurts most.'

'Well, I'm sure they don't do it on purpose. Later on we're going to look at birds in a way you haven't done before.'

'What way?'

'It's going to be a secret until you've finished your medicine and had your breakfast.'

'A secret! Does Daddy know it?'

'Nobody knows it but me so far. And if you're good then you can know it too.'

'A secret,' Jenny said reflectively. 'I don't really know any secrets.'

It took no time at all to administer the medicines and to give Jenny a quick bed bath.

Breakfast arrived—two trays, one for Jenny one for her. Minette smiled at Kelly, gave Jenny a quick kiss and then left. Kelly put her tray to one side for a moment and made sure that Jenny ate. A sensible breakfast for a little girl. A bowl of cereal, a fruit yoghurt, a bowl of freshly cut fruit salad. It looked appetising. But from behind Kelly came the smell from a cafetière of coffee. Now, that coffee was going to be good!

Just as Jenny finished her breakfast, Luc walked in the room. Kelly had been expecting him, known she'd have to see him, but his appearance still gave her a shock. Was she going to feel this way every time she saw him? It had only been eight hours or so since they had parted, but he looked somehow new, as if he was someone she was seeing for the first time—and he looked gorgeous.

'Daddy!' Jenny shouted. 'Daddy, Daddy.'

Luc smiled at Kelly. 'Good morning, Kelly. Did you sleep well last night? How are you feeling this morning?'

'Good morning, Luc. I'm feeling much better for all that sleep. Just a bit bruised and stiff.' She went on, 'I'll sit over here and eat my breakfast, you have a quick word with your daughter.'

She picked up her tray and took it to the far end of the room. Luc nodded his understanding. She was giving him time alone with his child.

Kelly sat at a little table, looking out of the window, she didn't want to look at Luc and Jenny. Be honest, she didn't want to look at Luc. The sight of him aroused so many conflicting emotions. She'd have to deal with them. Just what did she want?

Her breakfast, as she might have guessed, was wonderful. The coffee was far superior to the coffee she made (though it was in the same kind of cafetière). The croissants, she detected, were from the same baker she had used herself. Someone had been up early. It was a good breakfast, a pity she couldn't enjoy it more.

Finally she heard the scrape of Luc's chair, heard him saying goodbye to Jenny. She stood, walked across to him.

'Now, you're going to be good for Auntie Kelly aren't you?' Luc asked.

'Yes.' Jenny knew what she was going to say was important. 'Cos we've having a secret.'

'A secret?' Luc turned to Kelly, raised his eyebrows.

'Jenny will tell you her secret tonight,' Kelly said firmly. 'If she wants to, that is.'

'Well, I hope she will want to.' He kissed his daughter one last time.

'Before you go,' Kelly went on, 'this bed is on wheels. I'd like to wheel Jenny's bed outside for a while.'

'Wheel the bed outside? What a great idea! Why didn't I think of it? Kelly you're a genius, shall we do it now?'

'No. I need to be able to do it on my own. You go to work.'

'You will remember about sunblock? She's dark-haired but…'

'Luc! Where was I working last? In the desert. Don't talk to me about the dangers from the sun.'

'True. Sorry, I forgot. Now, you're sure everything is all right?' He looked at her, his gaze thoughtful, penetrating,

'Everything is fine. Jenny and Minette and I will get on very well together.'

She looked back at him, her eyes bold, defying him to question her further.

'Good. Then we will meet again at dinner.' He left and Kelly sighed with relief. For a moment there she thought he might have demanded to talk. And she just couldn't face it.

Minette came in to collect the trays and to talk about lunch. Kelly asked her to sit with Jenny a moment while she fetched a book from the living room. She had noticed it the night before. Then Minette left and Kelly turned to Jenny. 'Time for our secret now,' she said.

She'd checked that the wheels of the bed would easily unlock. And once unlocked it was so easy to push the bed outside. Jenny loved the ride. 'Now push me back in and then back out again,' she called.

'I don't think so,' said a slightly puffed Kelly.

Now for the secret. It had been a thought that had flashed across Kelly's mind as she'd listened to the dawn chorus. She pointed Jenny's bed towards the copse of trees at the bottom of the garden and then settled her upright with extra pillows. Then she ran into her own room, pulled something out of the bottom of her trunk. Something she had never used. Then she fetched herself a chair, returned to the side of Jenny's bed.

'The secret! You,' she said importantly, 'are going to become an ornithologist.'

Jenny's face filled with excitement and puzzlement. 'I am? What's that?'

'An ornithologist is someone who likes birds. You like birds, don't you?'

'Yes.'

'Well, we're going to look at all the birds in your garden and write down their names. And you're going to find them! With these!'

From behind her back Kelly produced her binoculars. They were lightweight and very powerful. Kelly adjusted the setting then handed them to Jenny.

'Look at the wood and see what you can see, Jenny!'

A few moments silence and then a squeal of delight. 'I can see the wood, it's so close I could touch it. And there's a bird!'

They had a good hour together and then, while Jenny was still enthusiastic, Kelly said that they had done enough of being an ornithologist for one day. They had seen three birds, found them in Luc's bird-spotters' book which Kelly had fetched from the living room and had written down their names. Jenny had learned to say 'ornithologist'. It had been a good start to the morning.

Kelly pushed the bed back inside, re-locked the wheels and then put Jenny's TV set on her bedside table. French children were just like English children. There were TV programmes that just could not be missed.

Minette had put two jugs of fruit juice in the little fridge in the room, one for Kelly, one for Jenny. No need to worry about Jenny for the next three-quarters of an hour, it was her favourite programme. Kelly poured herself a glass of freshly pressed orange juice and sat in an easy chair in a corner of the room. Looking after children was hard work.

Usually Luc enjoyed the twenty-minute drive along the quiet road to his surgery. There were odd glimpses of the sea, he could think about the day ahead or simply listen to his car radio. An easy time before work started.

Today was different. He had had a disturbed night. He had known Kelly for so little time. But during that time she had made an impression on him that no woman had ever made before. It wasn't just that physically she was gorgeous. Her ideas, her interests, her training all fascinated him. No, there was more to it than that.

As a doctor, a man who had seen more than his share of the good and bad in people, he couldn't explain it. When he looked at Kelly he just knew that there was something pulling their souls together. They belonged together. And he knew that she felt the same—though there was no way he could ever explain it. It was just so.

With a shudder, he realised that he had never felt this way about Merryl. And he had married her!

He had made some kind of decision. Whatever it was

between him and Kelly, it was serious. He had to press on—even thought he knew she had doubts. When he got to work he was slightly happier.

Kelly's day passed quickly and well. She enjoyed Jenny's company. Jenny was a typical little girl, usually happy in her life, curious about everything, but unable to concentrate on anything for too long. So for Kelly there was a constant need to find something new for them to do. But she liked it. It kept her busy, stopped her brooding about things.

They read, drew, looked for more birds, watched television, sang songs, talked about things. Minette kept them supplied with the most wonderful food and suggested that when Jenny had her afternoon sleep, Kelly might like to walk for an hour. So it was a good day.

But what would the night bring? What would it be like when Luc came home? She didn't really have time to think.

Minette told her what would be expected. Luc was working a long day at the surgery, he had phoned to say that he might be even later than usual. Jenny would be given her tea, have her wash and be ready to sleep. Then Luc would come in, read her a story and chat to her a while, and then wait till she went to sleep.

'He makes time for his daughter every day,' Minette said. 'Not just a few minutes, but a long time. He is a good parent.'

There had been emphasis on the 'he'. Evidentally Minette didn't think much of Merryl as a mother.

It went just as Minette had said. When Luc came in there was the usual heart-pounding moment. Just to see him, just to see him smile at her… But there was not the fear that she had felt that morning. They were still friends.

'You'll want to spend some time alone with Jenny,' she said. 'I've got a few things I need to do in my room.' She leaned over the bed, gave Jenny a kiss and said, 'See you in the morning, darling. Are you going to tell Daddy your secret?' And she was gone.

She'd enjoyed her day, but now she was just a little tired. She thought she'd stretch on the bed a while, Luc could find her here when he was ready. Say in half an hour…

Where was she? What was that knocking on the door? Why had she…? Kelly opened her eyes, blinked and focussed on the bedside clock. She'd been asleep for an hour! She rolled out of bed, stumbled over to the door and opened it. It was Luc.

'I'm sorry,' she gasped, 'I was asleep but I never sleep like this in the evening. I just…'

He smiled that gentle smile. 'You're still getting over yesterday. And looking after children is demanding work. I understand you have had a full day. Jenny too has gone to sleep quickly.'

'Good. And I've enjoyed being with her.'

'She has enjoyed being with you. But I am afraid you'll have to think of another secret for tomorrow. Now, we have an hour before supper. Shall I drive you over to the cottage so you can get what you might need over the next two weeks? You can leave some stuff there. I gather there's a lock on the small bedroom door.'

'Right.' There were things she needed to do in the cottage. Some things could be left, some food would have to be brought away, she needed clothes, books, her medical bag—there wasn't a lot to move. She had only brought a little with her.

When they got there, she shook her head as she saw the mess the cottage wall was in. The lorry had been towed away, builders had already erected some scaffolding and there were piles of bricks ready to be replaced. Inside, she sighed again. What had been her haven was now half wreck, half building site.

'I won't be long,' she said to Luc, 'I'll drive back myself in my own car? Why don't you go on ahead?'

He shook his head. 'I'll stay with you. I can see what you're feeling,' he said. 'You're sad. Some place that was particularly yours—it's been spoiled. It's almost as if you've been betrayed.'

'Yes,' she said after a moment. 'It's just like that.'

CHAPTER SEVEN

THE receptionist looked up as Luc entered the surgery. She seemed a little upset. 'Dr Laforge, Dr Briard says would you go to his room as soon as you arrive, please? There's something rather important to deal with.'

'Thank you, Renee.' Luc frowned. Not the kind of message he usually expected from his medical partner. Arrangements between them tended to be more casual. He hurried along to the room.

Paul Briard was in his consulting room, sitting on a chair, crouched over the sink. He didn't move as Luc entered.

'Paul, is anything wrong?' Luc walked to where he could see what Paul was doing, and winced. The sink was running red with blood. Paul was clutching his right forearm with his left hand, stopping blood from spurting from a deep cut in his wrist.

'Paul, we have a nurse here! Why didn't you call her?'

'She's out on a visit. Called in to say that she'd be delayed by half an hour. Luc, this is silly! I'm a doctor, I don't do this kind of thing! My shoelace was undone, I stood on it, fell over, put a hand out to save myself—and ripped it open on that picture on my desk.'

Luc glanced behind him. Paul had had a silver-framed picture of his wife and children on his desk. The frame and the shattered glass were now on the floor. There were blood stains too. 'Right Paul, for a start I want you on your back on your examination couch.'

Luc grabbed at the roll of paper that was used to cover the couch for each new patient. He tore off a large piece, wrapped it roughly round the still bleeding cut and said, 'That will stop you from bleeding over your clothes. Now, come over to the couch.'

He put an arm round Paul's waist, helped the man to stagger to the couch. Then he held the hand high to examine the wrist. 'At first sight there don't seem to be any glass fragments here. I'm going to put a temporary dressing on this, get you something warm and sweet to drink and then make a few arrangements.'

'I've got appointments in ten minutes!'

'Not this morning you haven't. In fact, I don't think you'll have any all day. You've lost too much blood.'

'But, Luc, I—'

'Paul, right now I'm the doctor and you're the patient. Be happy with that. Now, lie still.'

He went to the receptionist. 'Renee, check my appointments, and Dr Briard's. He won't be seeing anyone today, so I'll take over the more important ones. Will you look at all our patients and make me out a list of the most important? Then phone and cancel the rest. I'm going to take him a hot drink.'

'Yes, Dr Laforge. Is Dr Briard all right?'

'Just a cut,' said Luc.

Luc worked in a large, a well-equipped medical centre.

They were some distance from the nearest hospital. Sometimes it was necessary to perform tasks that were not really their job. Like now. Luc X-rayed the arm, checked for glass fragments. None. He sutured the cut, put Paul to bed in the tiny ward they had and erected a giving set to replace the lost fluids. It was good when you could be self-sufficient.

He had a full day—because of Paul's injury, much fuller than usual. He phoned to say that he would be late so could Minette or Kelly put Jenny to bed? And when he arrived home, Jenny was asleep and Minette said that Kelly had gone for a walk for an hour. Well, she was certainly entitled to time away from the house—but he had been rather looking forward to seeing her. So he showered, changed, sat in his living room, looking out across his sunlit garden, and poured himself a glass of red wine. He needed to relax. No, not relax. He needed to think about his life and how suddenly it had changed.

Feeling this way about a woman whom he had known for just over a week? He must be mad! But…he couldn't help it. Kelly had that effect on him. But what did he want of Kelly?

Deliberately, he made himself think of Merryl. He remembered the happiness he'd first had with her, the feeling of luck that he'd had when he'd thought she had chosen him. He remembered the things that, because he'd thought he was in love, he had chosen to ignore.

He had been on a year's secondment to a London hospital, where the work had been fascinating but non-stop. He'd had to work and study. Merryl hadn't understood that. If she'd wanted to go out, then he'd had to take her.

He had told himself that this was a sign of her devotion to him. The idea of selfishness had never crossed his mind.

Kelly was so different in her attitude to work. If it was there, it had to be done.

It wasn't Merryl's fault. It was just the way she was.

After he had parted from her he had been wary of all women. He had Jenny in his life, and that was enough. Or had been enough.

The attraction between Kelly and himself had been instant—but cautious. Both of them had been hurt, neither of them had wanted to chance love again. But something had made them. When he'd kissed her, it had said it all.

So what now? She had recognised the attraction between them—but in effect had asked for time. She needed time and Luc didn't care for inaction.

Of course, he knew that doing nothing was sometimes the only possible course of action. Some medical conditions you didn't try to treat until the time was right. Some quite painful diseases were not treatable, they just had to be left to run their course.

A good doctor knew this. But Luc hated it, he felt he was a man of action.

When he had been a soldier he had been told that, above all, he was not to be seen helping anyone. That would mean taking sides. But how could *any* person not try to stop suffering? Still, he had obeyed orders. That is, he had obeyed orders if he had been likely to get caught. His superiors had never known what he had managed on the quiet with his access to his small medical kit. Perhaps that's what had pushed him into becoming a doctor?

So how could he make Kelly love him more? Or just acknowledge the love that was there?

He sipped his wine, frowned. Was he considering manipulating her—as Merryl had manipulated him? That was not to be even thought of! At that moment Kelly entered the room. He walked across to meet her.

She was lovely. The formal dress she had worn to the *auberge*, the simple trousers and shirt that she wore at the moment, whatever she wore she was always lovely. He could tell that she had done a little something to her hair and her face but basically what he saw was pure, simple, lovely Kelly. For a moment he remembered her expression when he had knocked on her bedroom door the other evening. He had woken her, she had been still sleepy eyed when she'd answered. And the innocent smile she had greeted him with had told him a lot. She had been so happy to see him. She had not yet had the chance to put up her defences. But the defences were up now. Her smile was guarded, he would have to be careful.

'So good to see you, Kelly,' he said. 'May I pour you a glass of wine?'

'Please, but just a small one.'

He poured her a glass, gave it to her, and hoped she couldn't feel the trembling in his fingers as their hands touched. Just being in the same room as her brought him so much pleasure.

Kelly wasn't sure what she felt. The usual shock of his appearance whenever they met, the feeling of how good he looked, it was showing no sign of disappearing yet. What would it be like to spend another mealtime with him? She determined not to drink too much. Then honesty forced her to accept that the events two nights ago had not been due to alcohol. All had been her fault.

He led her to a corner of the room where windows opened onto the lawns and the copse beyond. They sat in two easy chairs and looked out. 'I've been looking at the birds,' he said. 'I've heard that Jenny was very enthusiastic about them and it made me enthusiastic too. Kelly, that was a brilliant idea.'

She felt pleased at the compliment. 'I enjoyed it as much as Jenny did,' she said.

'She wants to carry on with her birds' notebook. I thought—if you agree—that I might promise her a bird-spotters' book of her own.'

'When she's looked at them for a week or so. Let's make sure she's genuinely interested first.'

'Of course.'

There was something that Kelly had noticed. 'There seems to be a lot of birds in your garden,' she said, 'more than I would have expected. Certainly more than I've seen anywhere else.'

'Ah!' He smiled. 'They come to nest in my woods. As you know, France is a nation of hunters—and the hunters shoot birds whether they can eat them or not. But I will not permit shooting on my land, I have heard enough of the sound of guns. So the local hunters are upset but the birds seem to realise that this is a sanctuary and they flock here.'

Why doesn't that story surprise me? Kelly asked herself. It was a point of view with which she entirely sympathised. 'You don't approve of shooting?' she asked.

'For food and when it is necessary, yes. Shooting for sport, no.'

'I think I agree.' She said.

'We have a big garden here. I thought that in time, when she is old enough to appreciate them and old enough to look after them, I might buy Jenny some chickens. Minette could buy the eggs from her.'

'Now, that is a good idea.'

This was a nice, safe subject, Kelly thought. They could talk about a small child growing up without any too personal thoughts.

Behind them the door opened, and Minette's soft voice said, 'Dinner served now, m'sieur?'

'Please, Minette. I see you have already laid the small table.'

Luc stood, held out his hand to Kelly. 'Shall we dine, Kelly?'

'Let us do that, Luc.'

It was a simpler meal than the one they had had two nights before. A vegetable and lentil soup with herbs. A roast sea bass on a bed of vegetables. In the French manner, cheese before the pudding, which was crème caramel. And then there was fruit. There was little conversation throughout the meal, both seemed happy to eat and just comment on how wonderful the meal was.

Kelly felt more confident as the meal progressed. She was enjoying herself, being with Luc was not as strained as it might have been. There was something between them, in time it would have to be sorted out, but for now she just enjoyed his company. She had had—was having—a good day. When the meal was over they returned to the two chairs by the windows and Minette brought them coffee, two small glasses and a bottle of brandy.

Kelly was looking forward to a pleasant and peaceful evening when surprisingly Minette returned. 'There is a phone call for you, sir.'

Luc frowned. 'A phone call? Who rings at this time? I'm not on call.'

'The phone call is from London, sir. It is Madame Laforge, she says it is urgent.'

'She is Madame Laforge no longer, Minette! She is…I forget.' He stood, his anger only too obvious. 'I'll take the call in my study.'

He turned, said, 'Kelly, please excuse me.'

'It would be the height of bad manners not to answer, Luc. I'll sit here and drink coffee till you return.'

He left. Kelly found she had no wish to drink more coffee. She knew Luc was divorced, she had no doubt about his dislike for his ex-wife, but she wished that Merryl had not phoned. She knew from her break-up with Gary that almost as much pain could come from meetings after a parting than during it. There was always bitterness, on both sides. And with Gary, she had a growing certainty that he believed she was responsible for everything bad that happened.

Luc returned. 'Sorry about that, Kelly,' he said. 'These things are sent to try us.' As ever, his voice was calm, but Kelly could feel an underlying tension that made his words clipped and harsh.

He drank his now-cold coffee in one great mouthful. He reached for the brandy bottle, filled his glass and emptied that. Then he started to refill the glass but stopped when it was half-full.

'Whatever problems I have won't be solved by drinking too much,' he said.

'True.' Kelly allowed herself a small smile.

'Even divorced couples have to communicate at times,' he said, 'but this was the first time since the accident that I've spoken to Merryl directly.'

'I'm not surprised. Let me guess, you heard about the accident, you drove to where it occurred to find that Merryl had been drinking and Jenny was quite badly injured—you lost your temper with her.'

'I did. I said what I thought and Merryl was horrified and even a bit frightened. She said she saw a side of me that she'd never seen before.'

Luc leaned back in his chair, gazed at the ceiling. Casually he asked, 'Is it possible to love someone, even to be married to them, and not know what they are really like? Can you ever truly know another person?'

Kelly was suddenly alert. She glanced at Luc. His temper seemed to have vanished. This was not a casual question about his wife and his divorce. It was a question to her—and a difficult one.

'I thought I was in love with Gary. But then he turned out to be…well, not the man I wanted. And I realised after-wards that I'd known all about his bad points, known that he was shallow and self-centred and not even a very good actor. But I'd fooled myself because I wanted to be in love.'

'Shallow, self-centred and not a very good actor,' Luc said with a small smile. 'What would he say if he heard you describe him that way?'

'I can tell you exactly. He did hear, those are the words I used to him. He didn't like them—especially the bit about being a bad actor. He said I was boring and just didn't know how to have fun.'

'I don't find you boring. You rescue schoolchildren from buses and like paddling at night. So do you think you will ever be certain enough to fall in love again? Can you imagine finding the right man?'

Where was this conversation going? Kelly looked around her, almost in panic. She knew very well that this was not a vague, generalised question. He was asking her if she could ever love him. And at this moment she just didn't want to answer.

Unthinkingly, she reached for her own brandy glass, poured its contents into her mouth just as she was about to speak. She wasn't used to neat spirits, had only sipped in the past. This wasn't sipping! She choked, coughed, spluttered, leaned forward, desperately trying to get back her breath. She was aware of Luc pounding on her back—and laughing at the same time.

What a way to answer him!

'I'll fetch you some water,' he said, still smiling. 'You'll be fine in a minute.'

'I feel a fool,' she croaked.

But when he returned with the water and she had drunk it, she realised that choking on the brandy had given her a respite. She could alter the mock joking conversation of before, move onto a safer topic.

But the question echoed and re-echoed through her head. *Do you think you will ever be certain enough to fall in love again? Can you imagine finding the right man?* She didn't know what her answers would be. And she knew she'd like to ask him the same two questions.

Still… 'You say this is the first time that your ex-wife has been in touch since the accident? Not even to ask about Jenny?'

She looked up to see him smiling at her. He knew very well why she had changed the subject. But there was determination in his eyes. This was a topic that would be raised again.

However, she had asked a question, he would answer it. 'My ex-mother-in-law has phoned to ask once or twice. But no one has been to visit—thank goodness.' Then his expression changed as he snarled, 'Until now!'

'Your ex-wife is coming here to visit?' Kelly couldn't hide her alarm.

'She claims she wants some photographs of herself with Jenny. That is all. But she wanted to bring a professional photographer with her. If a professional photographer comes, those photographs will somehow find their way into the papers.'

'So you said she could not come?'

'No. She can come. She wouldn't say when but she's likely just to turn up in the next few days.' Luc paused a moment and then said, very deliberately, 'She also said that we have some personal things to sort out. I want to know what she means.'

This Kelly didn't like at all. And she saw that Luc was uneasy too.

'Luc, if your ex-wife is coming to visit, and you don't know when, I think that I should leave.'

'No! I will not have my life and Jenny's life messed up by that woman. It'll be hard enough for Jenny to have me and her mother together. You'll be the person that causes us all to behave.'

Jenny. Kelly hadn't thought of her. Her heart went out to a six-year-old confined to bed, warred over by two parents. She hadn't known her long, but she was getting to…like the little girl.

'Then I'll stay.' She thought a minute and then said, 'But the clothes of hers that I borrowed. I'll get them cleaned tomorrow, return them and you're never to say that I wore them.'

'Of course,' he said.

Next day she was due to visit the surgery for the first time and she felt apprehensive.

She travelled in with Luc and as they drove into the car park she looked approvingly at the building in front of her. For a start, it was very modern, obviously purpose built in a light grey stone with cream woodwork. It was single storey, the large windows now nearly all shuttered. Outside there were trees, shrubs, small flower-beds.

'This doesn't look like an English surgery,' she said. 'It's far too pretty.'

'If you are sick, injured or afraid, then a gloomy building can only make you feel worse. I want our surgery to be welcoming. Come and look round inside.'

A pleasant reception area, a smiling receptionist. 'Dr Laforge, Dr Briard asked to be told the minute you arrived.'

'Dr Briard is here?'

'He's made a special visit, to pick up his mail and to meet…to meet the new doctor.'

'Of course. Renee, this is Dr Blackwood.'

Feeling a bit shy, Kelly shook hands. She'd have to get out of this habit of being wary of meeting people!

But she took to Dr Briard at once. A burly man, older than Luc and whose English was not half as good. But he too smiled at her and she felt welcome at once.

Waving his bandaged wrist, Dr Briard said, 'I would like you to be my right 'and man—or woman.' He was obviously pleased with his little joke. 'Your room will be on the right of mine. Together we shall make a team.'

'I shall look forward to that. I prefer working as a team to working on my own.'

She had said that, trying to be polite. But when she had said it, she realised that it was true—she had always liked being part of a tight medical team. Only in the past year had she turned into a loner. And now she was changing back.

She was shown around the building. It was far more than a simple GP's surgery, there were facilities for quite advanced work. 'Sometimes we have to act quickly,' Luc explained, 'and it's a long way to the hospital.' She was told a little of the work she would be expected to do, shown her own little consultancy room which, as Dr Briard had said, was to the right of his room. 'And you can take all the English patients,' Dr Briard said hopefully. 'They like people to speak English. And when I have difficulty in understanding, they talk very fast and shout.'

'Not a good idea,' she agreed.

She was taken into the doctors' lounge, given a cup of coffee—the best coffee she had ever had in a medical institution. Then Luc and Dr Briard excused themselves and disappeared for a while. There were tax problems they had to discuss.

French doctors' lounges were just like English doctors' lounges, she decided. Just the coffee was better and the tattered magazines in French. She sat there, leafing through an old edition of a glossy magazine. She thought she would be happy here.

Then she heard a loud voice—a loud English voice. The voice was upset—and there was someone crying too. The lounge opened off the reception area. An English woman had come into reception and had a problem. Kelly told herself that it wasn't her problem, that she didn't work here yet, that someone would come and deal with the matter. But no one came.

Kelly sighed, stepped outside, looked at a red-faced, distracted-looking woman in a straw hat and a sleeveless dress. Clutching her leg was a crying little boy aged about seven.

'You've got to help me,' the woman was shouting at the receptionist. 'Roland here needs a doctor! He was just running and he fell over and put his hand out to save himself and look at his fingers! It's horrible! He needs an operation!'

'I'm a doctor. May I help?' Kelly said calmly.

'You're English!'

'May I see Roland's hand?'

The woman eased the crying boy away from her skirt, took his wrist and showed Kelly his hand. 'Look at that! It's horrible. I don't want to look.'

Kelly supposed that it did look horrible unless it was the kind of thing you were used to. Roland had dislocated two of his fingers. They stood up at right angles from the back of his hand.

'Nothing too serious,' she said to his mother. 'He's suffering more from shock than pain. We can deal with it easily. Now, if I can have a closer look…'

She lifted Roland to sit on the receptionist's desk. Then

she held the injured hand, ran her own fingers over the two dislocations. 'Look Roland!' she said suddenly. 'Can you see that big red bird outside?' She pointed through the glass doors.

It was the excitement in Kelly's voice that made him look, that made him, just for a second, forget his injured hand. Kelly held his palm in one hand, took the dislocated fingers on the other hand and pulled them back into place.

'Ooh!' shouted Roland. But it was a cry of shock rather than pain.

'All done.' Kelly smiled at the mother. 'In a moment Dr Laforge will be here and—'

'Do we have a problem?' Drs Laforge and Briard appeared.

Just like buses, Kelly thought. You wait when you need one and when you've stopped needing one they turn up in masses. She said, 'This is Roland. He dislocated two fingers and I've just slipped them back into their sockets. I thought a cold compress and perhaps a check to see that nothing else… Sorry, you're the doctors here.'

'We're all doctors here,' said Luc, 'but I'll deal with this little boy for now. Paul, want to have a coffee with Kelly? This won't take long.'

'Of course.'

Paul escorted Kelly back into the lounge. 'Medicine can be exciting, can't it?' he asked.

'I've been excited in my time,' she replied.

Because Paul was not able to use his right hand Kelly offered to start work the next afternoon. Everyone thought this a good idea. She took her own car into work as she would be working very different hours from Luc. Which would mean she could still spend time with Jenny.

It was agreed that technically she would be Paul's assistant. He was supposed to check all her prescriptions, agree any treatment that she thought necessary, sign the vast number of forms. In fact, as he told her, he intended to do no such thing. 'This is a paper thing only,' he said. 'I have every faith in you.'

It was a different kind of medicine from that which she had last practised. A lot of the work was to do with seeing patients—often older patients—who had long-standing conditions and who needed regular check-ups. She found that her French was quite good enough for the chat that was apparently part of the therapeutic regime. The ratio of doctors to patients was much higher in France than in England. There was always time for a few words.

She was also sent most of the British patients. Here again, talk was nearly as important as medicine. Many were gastric complaints. A change in water perhaps, or too much rich food. Easy enough to reassure and treat. But there was another complaint that made it difficult for her to keep her temper—surely everyone knew by now? Excessive sunlight was dangerous. The adults had only themselves to blame. She treated them, of course, but tried to impress on them— firmly but politely—the dangers of excessive sunbathing. But when one baby was brought in, bright red from the sun, she did lose her temper. Not shouting and raging, that wasn't her way. 'Do you realise,' she said, in an apparently calm voice, 'that if you had left your little girl in the sun for another ten minutes she could have died? And the French are far less lenient about things like this than the British.'

'Well, we thought—' the father started in an aggressive voice.

But Kelly had just smelled the alcohol on his breath. 'You thought? I doubt that. If you tried to think more and drink less, your poor baby wouldn't be in this state. Now, good afternoon. If the little girl appears to be any worse, bring her back here at once.'

Later she thought about what she had said and wondered if she had gone too far. So she confessed to Luc—and he laughed. 'The joke,' he said, 'is that the parents would take that from an English doctor. If I had said it they'd think I was just some awkward foreigner.'

'Too much sun is not good. People need to know that,' she muttered.

'You're thinking of your life in the desert?'

'I've had patients die of heat prostration. Not pretty.'

'But I'll bet you saved some.' He reached out, stroked the back of her neck. Then he suddenly pulled his hand away. That was not permitted. But she felt sorry.

There were a surprising number of people coming in with cuts—especially fishermen with cuts to the hands. This upset Paul. With one of his hands still bandaged he was incapable of the delicate task of suturing. The first time he had a patient with a cut, he asked Kelly to step in to offer her advice. 'It's a really bad cut. I just can't do this, Kelly. I could wait until Luc is ready but he has a long list today.'

'You have a treatment room here, I can see to this there.'

Paul didn't know all of Kelly's story, he knew only that she was a doctor. But Kelly was a very good doctor. And she had spent months cutting, cleaning, probing, suturing flesh that had been blasted and torn apart. A hand badly gashed by a giant hook on a fishing line was no great problem.

This was only a GP's surgery. But it was nearly a hundred and forty kilometres to the nearest large hospital, so the surgery was equipped with quite a sophisticated treatment room. Occasionally it was used by the local midwives, and both Paul and Luc had performed minor surgery there. Kelly had looked around it before, had approved of what she had seen. There was a variety of the simpler surgical tools, even a machine for general anaesthesia. Kelly felt instantly at home here.

Paul watched, astounded, as Kelly ring-blocked the hand, cleaned the cut, pulled the edges together, and secured them with tiny sutures. 'Kelly, that was amazing,' he whispered. 'And you were so quick!'

'Sometimes you have to be quick.'

For her this had been a minor operation. But she remembered times when there had been a line of men waiting, in the heat, for similar operations. It had been necessary to be quick.

She worked three afternoons and found she was thoroughly enjoying herself.

It was her fourth afternoon at the surgery, she was getting into the swing of things. Today Luc was away on a course, Paul and she were the two doctors in charge. Things went well until it was nearly time for her to leave. Then she heard shouting from the reception area, the sound of someone panicking. A moment later Paul knocked on her door, came in at once. 'We have a problem,' he said. 'A man has been knocked down by a car, not half a kilometre away. They didn't send for SAMU, they loaded him into the car, brought him here, he's in the treatment room now. He's conscious, he can walk but—'

'What's the problem?'

'He can't breathe properly. The car hit him in the face and neck, there's damage to the respiratory tract. I think there's swelling there and it's getting worse. His trachea is closing up Kelly. I tried the Heimlich manoeuvre on him three times—no result at all.'

Kelly shook her head in dismay. The Heimlich manoeuvre was simple but often a lifesaver. You stood behind the patient, wrapped your arms round him so your hands were clasped over his abdomen and jerked your hands backwards. If there was an obstruction in the trachea, the shock sometimes dislodged it. This time it hadn't worked.

'Can you work as an anaesthetist?' she asked Paul.

'I've been on a course, I can operate a simple machine like the one we have.'

'Right. We're going to perform a tracheotomy on this man. Let's get him prepped.'

'But Kelly, that is an operation beyond us doctors. And, anyway, there is no way I could hold a scalpel. I could—'

'I'm a surgeon, not just a doctor. You do the anaesthetic and I'll cut.'

'A surgeon? Where?'

'That doesn't matter now. Let's get started!'

Paul looked at her in bewilderment for a moment. Then he nodded and said, 'If we don't operate the man could die. We could perform an emergency tracheotomy but—'

'But indeed,' Kelly said. 'There'll be no emergency medicine here. This is a surgery.'

There were stories of emergency tracheotomies, of

tracheas being cut open with a penknife, of the barrel of a ballpoint pen being used as a clear airway. They were true stories. But Kelly wanted no part of that.

By now their patient was having great trouble in breathing and was showing all the signs of distress she would have expected. His face was cyanosed, the efforts he was making to breathe were painful to hear. Kelly recognised the pain, could feel for the man, but switched off any emotional reaction. She would be most useful here if she was calm, collected.

First, a lightning check. The man had been brought in suffering from injuries to the face and neck. That was not to say that there were no other injuries. Together, Kelly and Paul examined the man. Nothing further. Good.

The patient was placed on the table. Paul acted as nurse, isolating the neck and chest with sterile drapes and then disinfecting the skin. Then he moved to the anaesthesia machine. Kelly nodded. 'Put him out,' she said. A quick injection and the patient was unconscious.

Kelly had scrubbed up, was masked and gowned, had put on the rubber gloves. She took a scalpel from the sterile pack and leaned over the patient.

This was the first time she had been a surgeon in a long time. A tiny part of her mind detached itself, looked down on her standing there, scalpel in hand. Just how well would she do? This would be interesting.

Other surgeons had told her that the very first cut was the worst. To see an area of apparently perfect flesh, to slice your scalpel across it so the blood runs out... But after that things got easier.

Halfway between the Adam's apple and the tip of the

breastbone. Kelly found the place, made the first cut. There were the neck muscles. Carefully she separated them, probed under them. The thyroid gland—she cut it down the middle. And there were the rings of cartilage that made up the trachea. Kelly cut into the tough wall. There was a whistling sound as the patient took his first full breath.

Kelly had a sterile tracheotomy tube ready, she slid it into the opening and then carefully stitched it into place. Then the opening was closed and a dressing placed round it.

She looked up at Paul. 'All done,' she said. 'Bring him round. Now we can phone for an ambulance and get this man off to a proper hospital where he can have that face and jaw looked at.'

Paul worked at the anaesthesia and together they heaved the patient up so that he was half sitting. The best position to recover from an anaesthetic. 'I've already phoned for the ambulance, it won't be too long. Though it would have been too long for this man if it hadn't been for you. And you could see to the jaw and face if you wanted. I could see the skill there.'

Kelly lifted a corner of the temporary dressing and glanced at the injuries. 'I could do a first job,' she said, 'but I suspect he's going to need plastic surgery. That's not what I do.'

'What is a first-rate surgeon like you doing working part time in a GP's surgery?'

'It's a long story,' Kelly said.

Just at that moment the ambulance arrived. Kelly let Paul give the report on the patient's condition and treatment, deal with the little bit of paperwork. Then the patient was gone. He was no longer her responsibility.

'Excuse me a minute,' Kelly said. She went to the ladies'
cloakroom, looked at herself in the mirror and smiled. She
recognised that confident face.

Now she was certain that the old Kelly was back.

CHAPTER EIGHT

KELLY enjoyed herself working in the afternoons, enjoyed herself just as much being with Jenny in the mornings. It struck her that she'd never had much to do with children. Not only her work but her social life had kept her from being closely involved with the upbringing of a child. And she had no relatives with nieces or nephews.

She had never talked about having a family with Gary, most of Gary's conversation had been about Gary. But now it struck her that having children was largely the point of getting married. She had never thought much about it but now…would she like a family? Yes, she would, she decided.

The next thought was inevitable. Luc and Jenny were inseparable, they would come as a package. And she loved them both so it was…

That was enough of that kind of thought.

Jenny was an intelligent child so she needed to be kept interested. In anything. She grew more and more irritated by the fact that she was confined to her bed, and it took all Kelly's powers of imagination to work out new ways of keeping her calm and busy. They had a lot of fun studying birds. But there had to be more than that. There was music and drawing and craftwork…

'This child of mine is going to be a genius,' Luc said one evening when he discovered Kelly and Jenny had just constructed an origami dragon. 'Kelly, you have shown her so many new skills.'

'This child of yours reminds me of you,' Kelly retorted. 'She won't let anything pass without examination. I've never heard so many questions. "Why can't humans fly?" Try answering that to a six-year-old.'

'But you like Jenny asking you questions. You always smile when you think of an answer.'

Kelly realised that this was true. She was also both pleased and shocked to realise that Luc had noticed so much about her. 'I do,' she said. 'It's because for quite a while no one asked me anything. Largely because I wouldn't answer.'

'That time has passed.'

He turned to where Jenny was carefully colouring her dragon green. 'Jenny, I have brought a DVD to show you.'

'I've had my television time for today,' Jenny said sadly. Luc raised his eyebrows at Kelly.

'We only watch so much television each day,' she explained. 'In the morning we negotiate what we're going to see.'

'That is remarkable. When Jenny's mother was… At one time that television set seemed never to be off.'

Kelly decided not to ask questions. Luc's relationship with his ex-wife was none of her affair. But she did feel rather pleased that Luc approved of what she was doing. 'What is the DVD about?' she asked.

He showed her. 'I ordered it from the library,' he said.

Kelly looked. It was a copy of a programme first shown on French TV, dealing with the commonest French birds. 'I think that we can consider this bird time, not television time,' she said.

The next day was a special day—or a special night. Luc came home with a wheelchair! It was specially adapted so that Jenny's injured leg could rest straight. 'We think that the bones in Jenny's leg will have knitted sufficiently for her to risk being moved,' Luc explained. 'But can you and Minette lift her from bed to wheelchair?'

'No, we can't. But I can lift her on my own.' Kelly flexed the biceps of her right arm. 'Feel that!'

He did feel it—gently. And she liked it.

So Kelly felt very happy at her work—in fact, happier than she had ever been in her life. But how did she feel about Luc? He had not kissed her as he had that night on the beach—but the memory of what she had felt didn't fade. She suspected it hadn't faded for Luc either. At times she caught him looking at her and in his eyes there was a sadness or a longing that she recognised. She felt it too.

And it was awkward, living in his house. Certainly they were together a lot, enjoying each other's company. But they had made an agreement and Kelly knew that he would never try to kiss her again when she was a guest in his home. It would upset his sense of honour. But what if she were to kiss him…?

Because of Jenny she spent a lot of time with him and so came to know him better. She came to like him more and more. He had a quiet sense of humour, dedication to his job. She told herself that liking and loving were two dif-

ferent feelings, that she was entitled to like but that love
was not for her. Still, telling the difference between the two
was often difficult.

She saw how much he loved his daughter. He spent as
much of his time as possible with her. Kelly saw the way
his face lit up when Jenny caught sight of him. 'Jenny
doesn't really need me,' she told him. 'You and Minette
give her all the love and attention she needs.'

'I can't imagine how any parent wouldn't want to spend
as much time as possible with their child. It is a joy to me
like few others.'

'Six is an enchanting age anyway,' Kelly said. She
realised that he was talking about his ex-wife, her lack of
interest in her daughter. As ever, there had been real bitterness in his voice.

On Friday night he said, 'To celebrate, shall we go out
for dinner again tonight? You have hardly been out all week.'

'I'd like that,' she said after a moment. 'But could we
go somewhere other than L'Auberge de la Rivière?'

'That might be a good idea.'

The night at the restaurant was in her thoughts con-
stantly. She thought she would never forget it. She suspected that Luc felt the same way.

He took her to dinner in the Café des Amis, a town-centre
restaurant that was completely different from the one they
had visited a week before. It was more crowded, noisier,
there were more large parties. People came here to have a
good evening with their friends. As they were shown to
their table, three or four people waved at Luc, he was obviously well known.

'You brought me here because the atmosphere is the complete opposite of L'Auberge de la Rivière,' she said.

He didn't deny it. 'The food is just as good. L'Auberge is wonderful in its way but it's a quiet place. You're coming out into the world now, you will be mixing more with people.'

'I suppose so.'

For a moment she gazed into his eyes and knew that both of them were thinking the same thing. Last week had been magic. After the meal and the paddling, the kiss had meant so much. Stopping it, breaking off, had been harder, more painful, than almost anything she could remember. And now she realised she felt a little selfish. It had hurt him as much as it had hurt her.

A moment or two of silent communion. Then he said, 'This place is famous for its oysters. Would you like to start with a dozen?'

'Sounds good to me.' Decision made. They were here to enjoy themselves, not muse over what might have been.

The food was very good and Kelly enjoyed herself. One or two people came over to say hello to Luc, to be friendly but also obviously curious about who she was. He introduced her as Dr Blackman from England, who would be working with him. This didn't satisfy most people, but Luc was not going to say any more.

Then there was a surprise. They were just about to order coffee when a voice said, 'Now, who would have expected this. We were just passing, looked through the window and here you are.'

Kelly looked up. It was Paul and an attractive smiling woman who was presumably his wife.

Luc stood. 'Paul! You're too late for dinner but we were about to have coffee and a brandy. Will you join us?'

'With pleasure. And I want to introduce Madeleine here to my new right hand. Madeleine, this is Dr Blackman.'

'Please, call me Kelly,' said Kelly, shaking hands.

'And I am Madeleine.'

A waiter fetched two chairs, and coffee and brandy ordered. It turned out that Paul and Madeleine were just walking back from the harbour, they had been to look at the sunset. Kelly already had decided that she liked Paul— he had a sense of humour, was easy to work with. And she found herself liking Madeleine even more.

'You three are doctors, I am the owner and designer of a dress shop,' Madeleine pronounced. 'So three-quarters of the time we will talk about medicine, one quarter of the time we will talk about dresses.'

'But we men know nothing about dresses,' Luc complained.

Madeleine beamed. 'Then sit silently and learn.'

In fact, they talked about a dozen things, from politics to the best way to bring up children. After a couple of minutes of initial shyness Kelly found herself enjoying the conversation no end. It struck her that it had been months since she had sat with a group of similarly minded friends and…just talked.

So they talked. After quite a while Madeleine stood and said, 'I can see you two men are looking restless. There's something to do with work that you have to discuss. Fair enough. For just five minutes Kelly and I will go to make ourselves even more beautiful and you two can plot in our absence. Come, Kelly!' With a smile Kelly followed Madeleine to the ladies'. She liked her new friend.

The Café des Amis had an unusually luxurious restroom. Kelly sat side by side with Madeleine and the two of them stared at their reflections in the gilt-framed mirrors in front of them. 'It is good to see Luc out with a new lady,' Madeleine said, 'especially one as attractive as you. He has been alone for too long. Perhaps his wife did put him off women, but that must pass!'

Kelly shook her head. 'We're not together in that sort of way,' she said. 'We both know that we're friends, not lovers. I look after his daughter, I'm doing some work at the surgery. But that is all.'

'Friends, not lovers, indeed!' Madeleine snorted. 'I have seen the way he looks at you when he thinks no one will notice. And I have seen the way you look at him when you think no one will notice. I design and make dresses for women, Kelly, I can tell what they want before they know themselves.'

'Well, we are good friends,' Kelly said weakly, 'but I assure you, that is all.'

'That may be all for now,' Madeleine said with assurance. 'But we will see what the future brings. Now, shall we go back?'

Luc took her back shortly after that. Kelly knew that both of them were thinking of the previous week, of what had happened at the end of the promenade—of the kiss. But neither said anything about it. Their conversation was light-hearted, but both were aware of the thoughts that they just could not voice.

When they got back Kelly refused a nightcap, said she was tired, she'd like to go to bed at once.

'Of course,' Luc said. 'Did you enjoy your evening? Did you enjoy the company of Madeleine and Paul?'

'Very much so. They seem a happy couple.'

'They are. They have the kind of marriage I should like to have. Goodnight, Kelly.'

'Goodnight, Luc.' Kelly fled. She had enjoyed the evening very much. But the end of it seemed curiously anti-climactic. Just what did she want?

It was Saturday. Luc was at home all day. 'Being with Jenny is as much fun as ever,' Kelly told Luc. 'We're carrying on with the bird notebook, we've started to read more and we're getting an interest in music. But she's getting better and she's getting irritated. She's started to feel that there are things missing in her life. We go out in the morning in the wheelchair but she needs to mix with other children of her age.'

Luc nodded. 'I am aware of that. But all her school-friends are away, it is the holidays.'

'Don't you know anyone we could invite round? If not friends, then family?'

He thought a moment. 'I have a sister, Clarice, who lives about a hundred and twenty kilometres away. She has one child, a serious little boy called Marcel, who is about two years older than Jenny. The two of them get on very well.'

'That's perfect! Could they come to see us? Just for half a day?'

She looked at the expression of doubt in his face. 'There's some reason why not?'

He seemed to make up his mind. 'Clarice cannot move from the house. Her husband is at home recovering from a…from a badly broken leg and she will not leave him.'

Kelly had noticed his doubt. 'What's the full story, Luc? You're holding something back from me.'

He sighed. 'Clarice's husband is a soldier. There are photographs of him in uniform all over the house. His leg was broken by a bullet and I thought this knowledge might upset you. It might bring back your fears.'

'It won't upset me. I've had shrapnel in my leg, we can swap stories. But thanks for thinking of me.'

She wondered if he knew how easy it now was for her to joke about this. She also wondered if he knew just how much he and Jenny had helped her. She went on, 'So would she like us to call? You've brought that new wheelchair home for Jenny, we can easily fit it into the car.'

He smiled. 'I am sure Clarice would like to see us.'

He phoned, they were to go to visit Clarice and Marcel the very next day. Jenny was greatly excited—she hadn't been out of the house for too long. 'Marcel will be impressed by my bird book, won't he?' she asked.

'I'm sure he will. You must take your notebook to show him as well.'

'I like Marcel. He tells me things.'

The trip was a definite success. Marcel and Jenny were old friends, they got on together at once. With great care Marcel pushed Jenny in her wheelchair down the garden and Jenny pointed out a few birds to Marcel, who took careful note. Luc went upstairs to talk to his brother-in-law, but Clarice asked if Kelly didn't mind if she wasn't invited to meet him. 'He is having one of his bad days,' she said. 'His wound is healing—slowly—but at times he is not himself. I think it is because he had been confined to his bed for so long.'

'I can understand that,' Kelly said.

It was a good day. Clarice served tea on the lawn, and when Luc was at the other end of the garden, playing with Jenny and Marcel, Clarice said, 'I am glad that Luc has met you. And you are a better mother to Jenny than his wife ever was.'

'We're just friends,' Kelly said, and ignored Clarice's meaningful smile. What was this? Everyone seemed to be pairing her off with Luc. This was the second woman in the week who had mentioned it. Still…it was nice to have her work with Jenny appreciated.

She thought about Jenny as she sat in the back of the car with her as Luc drove them back. Jenny held Kelly's hand for the first ten minutes and then she went to sleep. She was getting really fond of the little girl. No, she was getting to love her. It wasn't only adults who could love. But it was impossible to think of Jenny without thinking of Luc. They were a package. Was it a package that she wanted? She felt dissatisfied with herself. She felt that she had to make some kind of a decision about Luc.

Minette had gone to visit relations but had left food on the kitchen table. Kelly tried to feed a drowsy Jenny, but all Jenny wanted was to sleep. So Kelly put her to bed while Luc went to get changed.

When she came back she found Luc staring at what Minette had put out. 'I asked for a light supper,' he said. 'Does this look like a light supper?'

'It's not very light, is it? But it all looks delightful. Shall we load a tray each and go to sit in the living room? It'll be like a picnic.'

'Sounds good.'

'Remember how the headmistress sent me a bottle of champagne for helping the children? Well, I brought it here. Minette put it in your cellar for me. I said we'd have to share it. Shall we have it now? I noticed you didn't drink much at Clarice's because you'd be driving.'

She saw his face light up with pleasure. 'What a great idea! Kelly, you're a wonder.'

He walked to the cellar door and almost casually dropped a kiss on her cheek as he passed her. Just a friendly kiss. But she loved it more than perhaps he knew.

They ate their supper in the living room, and Kelly took the dishes back to the kitchen. When she returned Luc had drawn the curtains, had moved to the couch and carried the two glasses and the champagne to the coffee-table. Normally Kelly would have sat opposite him in the great easy chair. This evening she sat beside him. Something told her that it was time.

He poured them a glass of champagne, lifted his and clinked his glass against hers. 'Who shall we drink to?'

'Well, this was given to us because two passing doctors happened to help some young girls. So let's drink to them. That is, to us.'

'To us,' toasted Luc, and raised his glass to hers. Their fingers touched. The smallest of contacts but she trembled at it.

The bubbles tickled her throat, the wine was chill on her tongue. What more could a woman ask but to be sitting drinking champagne with a wonderful man whom she… whom she what? She put down her glass, moved nearer to Luc, leaned her head against his shoulder. 'I feel tired, but happy,' she said. 'No special reason. I just do. Life seems good to me.'

It seemed the obvious thing for him to stretch his arm round her shoulders, pull her to him. 'It seems good to me too,' he murmured.

'Have you found the past few days hard? Living with me and just…well, just living with me?'

She looked up to see his grin. 'Very hard. I know we agreed not to, but every time I see you I want to…well, you know.'

'I know what you mean. You know I've found it hard too?'

'Well, in that case…'

'Luc!' She tried to sound stern, to sound disapproving, but it didn't come out that way.

He grinned. 'I just want to hold you. Just pull you close to me, and you can put your head on my shoulder.'

'All right,' she said. 'But that's all.'

She knew she didn't mean it and so did he. His head bent over hers, he kissed her gently, as she knew he would. One of his hands stroked the back of her head. He pulled her to him so she could feel the warmth of his body. She thought she could stay like this for ever.

Then for ever seemed to be too long. Perhaps it was the way he was kissing her, tiny kisses feathering over her face, along her neck. This was wonderful but she felt—she needed—something more.

And when had they moved? She'd thought they were sitting side by side so how come she was now lying on her back—with him gently undoing the buttons on her shirt, pushing the cloth aside, kissing her shoulders, the swell of her breasts and…how had he undone her bra?

But she liked it so much! She pulled him to her, opened her lips to his insistent tongue, felt the warmth travel down her body, telling her that this was only a beginning, that there must be more. He took his lips from hers, his head plunged downwards so he could take the hard peak of her breast into his mouth. 'Luc I want…I need you, I want… Will you…?'

'Daddy?' A tiny wavering voice came from the child alarm in the corner.

'Daddy?' This was not the voice of a child who was half-asleep.

'Where are you, Daddy?' Now there was the threat of tears.

It was a hard thing to do. Kelly put her hands on his shoulders, eased him backwards. 'You have to go,' she said, 'you know that.'

'But, Kelly, I… We…'

'You have to go. I'll still be here when you come back.'

He stood, pulled his unbuttoned shirt back together. 'Wait for me,' he said. One hard swift, passionate kiss. And he was gone.

For a while Kelly just lay there, reliving what she had just gone through—and dreaming about what she had expected, and wanted. But then she shook herself. She sat upright, fastened her bra, buttoned up her shirt. She needed to think.

She had gone too far. Desperately, she had wanted to carry on to the inevitable end of what they had been doing. But now she had time to pause, to think.

She was scared. She had wanted to give herself to Luc, finally and totally—but she was scared. She remembered how she had felt when Gary had thrown her over so brutally. Of course, Luc wasn't Gary. But she had known Gary longer and still been amazed by what he had done to her.

What was she to do?

She stood, looked at herself in the mirror. It seemed to her that what she had just been doing would be obvious to anyone who saw her. Good thing Minette wasn't around.

Luc would be back in a moment, she could only guess what he would want—well, who could blame him? And it was what she wanted too, she thought.

But she was frightened. Frightened of what she would feel if all this fell apart. But how could she do this to Luc?

Only one thing. She would try to explain to him. She knew he would be bitterly disappointed—well, so was she. But she trusted he would understand.

And before she could consider further, he was back in the room.

He came to her, took her in his arms and kissed her. At first she relaxed—but then remembered this was not what she had decided and her body stiffened. He felt it at once. 'Kelly, sweetheart, what is it?'

'Let's sit down, Luc.'

She would try to explain, she hoped he would understand. And she knew that her behaviour could be seen in the worst of terms. When she looked at him she saw an expression of sadness, of resignation. And that was harder to bear than anger would have been.

'You know I've been ill—well, I'm over that. I'm still a bit underconfident because of Gary but that's coming back. And you know about Gary dropping me so cruelly. Well, I'm not over that. I'm over him, I can see him for what he is now. But I still am fearful of giving myself to anyone. It seems to be too great a risk! I know it's wrong and I know it hurts you but I can't help it!'

'The last thing I want to do is hurt you,' he said gently, and that made her feel worse.

'I'm going to bed now. But I'm going to make you an offer, a promise. Next week we'll carry on as if nothing had happened. Say nothing about this to each other. But next Sunday either I'll go to bed with you or I'll move out of here and only see you at work. Please, Luc, I need this time!'

His was a sad smile. 'If that's what you want. Do you know how much I'm waiting for and dreading next Sunday?'

'About as much as me,' she said.

On Monday morning Paul came to sit by her while she was having a coffee in the doctors' lounge. 'I don't know if you want to hear this,' he said, 'but I want to tell you. We had a note from the hospital where our tracheotomy patient was taken. The surgeon there sends his compliments and says it was some of the best suturing he has ever seen, and if you ever want a position you can come and work with him.'

'Well, that's nice,' Kelly said. She felt a faint stirring of pride—the first for a long time.

'So are you thinking of becoming a surgeon again?'

'At the moment I'm quite enjoying what I am doing,' Kelly said. 'I like working here.'

And she was. The work at the surgery, the mornings with Jenny, the pleasure she took in Luc's company—all made for a happy life. She ought to be happier than she could remember. But there was Luc to consider. What was her relationship to be with him? She still didn't know.

* * *

Luc broached something new when they had dinner together that night. 'On Saturday next Jenny and I have been invited to a wedding,' he said. 'In fact, it is Minette's granddaughter who is getting married. Jenny was very much looking forward to it. Children have an important part to play in weddings. Madeleine Briard has made her a special dress with what Jenny called a big twirly skirt.' Luc sighed. 'I am afraid she will not be able to twirl very much in her wheelchair.'

'She's a happy child, she'll have a lovely time,' Kelly said.

'I am sure she will. She would enjoy it even more if you were with her. So both she and I want you to come to the wedding. And so does Minette, she asked me to ask you.'

'A wedding?' Kelly considered. Even a fortnight ago, the thought of going to a wedding would have been hard. She would have remembered her own plans, then the letters she had to write, the dress she had to give away… but now, why not?

Luc seemed to misunderstand her hesitation. 'Perhaps I should have made it more clear, you will be working. The groom is an old friend of mine, I have assorted duties to perform. And while I am doing so there will be no one to look after Jenny.'

She looked at him suspiciously. 'Luc Laforge, I just do not believe that. Jenny will be surrounded by friends. You are trying to blackmail me into coming.'

'That is true. I plead guilty. I am ashamed of myself.'

'Then you shouldn't be trying to hide a smile. All right, I'd love to come.' Then she thought. 'But it's only five days away! Luc, I don't have anything to wear. I've bought some new dresses but nothing suitable for a wedding!'

Luc smiled the smile of the man who has considered every eventuality. 'I thought of that,' he said. 'In another half-hour we will be having two guests for an evening drink—Paul and Madeleine. And Madeleine will be bringing a selection of dresses, all in your size, all suitable for a wedding. You are to borrow one.'

'Right,' Kelly said faintly.

It was good to see Madeleine again so quickly. The four sat in the living room while Luc poured wine and Minette brought in a selection of canapés. As before, they chatted about anything and everything—and Kelly was reminded again of how good it was just to sit with a group of friends and talk. She was doing more of it lately and she liked it.

And after twenty minutes Madeleine rose and said, 'You men can sit here and talk about man things. But Kelly and I have more important things to discuss. Come, Kelly, we will go to your bedroom. We have a dress to choose.'

'Perhaps we men would like to see the selection,' Luc suggested.

'You can't. Your comments would only distract us. Perhaps when the choice is made…we shall see. Your function will be to agree that the dress is wonderful.'

This might even be fun, Kelly thought.

It *was* fun. From the car Madeleine brought four dresses, each covered in transparent plastic. Carefully, she laid them side by side on Kelly's bed.

'You are not to outshine the bride,' she said. 'But for a wedding you must dress up. There must be a sense of occasion. The other guests must look at you and think, That woman is chic! Your dress must not be too revealing, neither must it be too prim. To show how happy you are for the bride and groom you must show that you have come at your well-groomed best, and you are supremely confident in your appearance.'

Supremely confident? Kelly thought. Now, that will be a laugh. But she merely said, 'It sounds a lot to manage.'

'You have the face and the figure. My dress will do the rest. Now…all these will fit you. No need for measurements, I am a dressmaker, I know sizes.' Madeleine unzipped the plastic covering of the four dresses. 'Which would you like to try on first?'

Kelly looked at the dresses. Once I would have considered going to a wedding in my army dress uniform, she thought, and I'd have been proud to do so. Then she realised that that life was behind her. Mentally, she shrugged. Time to get on with the future.

For the first time she looked carefully at the dresses. And her mind was made up at once. 'I want to try them all on,' she said, 'and I'll think about each one. But I'll try that one last and I know it'll be the one I pick.'

Madeleine knew when not to comment. 'Let's get started, then.'

It was amazing what effect trying on the dresses had on her. It lifted her spirits tremendously. The first thing she realised was that Madeleine was indeed a brilliant dressmaker. Each of the first three dresses she tried on fitted her perfectly. Each of them had the right design, the right fabric, the right cut and line. She would have been pleased and proud to wear any one of them. But the fourth one…

A pale turquoise creation in silk, with spaghetti straps

and a fitted top that flattered her figure. A long skirt, cut on the bias and with sufficient freedom so she could walk easily. And there was a wrap in a darker turquoise with a silver thread running through it.

'Yes,' Madeleine said thoughtfully, 'that does something for you. You'll need a strapless bra, of course, but you can buy one of those easily. Now, stand there and admire yourself. Don't take it off. I'll be back in exactly five minutes.'

In fact Kelly found it easy to do as she was told. The dress did so much for her! So for five minutes she admired herself.

Madeleine returned with a small box. 'You could wear a big hat,' she said, 'but I think we want to show that face of yours. So how about this?'

Kelly peered inside. A tiny confection of black lace and feathers. 'It's a fascinator,' she cried. 'I've never worn one in my life before.'

Madeleine placed it carefully on her head. 'You'll look well in this. Now see yourself in the mirror. What do you think?'

'I think I need new shoes,' said Kelly.

CHAPTER NINE

SOME small, womanly things gave her much pleasure. One morning she took Jenny into town so they could go on a shopping expedition together. Somehow she fitted the wheelchair into her car and they set off for Merveille. Madeleine had given her a list of suitable boutiques.

First there were shoes to buy—strappy sandals, Madeleine had suggested. There would be quite a bit of walking and certainly dancing afterwards. And at the first shop they visited she found just the right thing, in a black kid leather. Comfortable, right for walking or dancing, with just enough of a heel to make them elegant. Happily, Kelly bought them at once. 'Aren't we going to look in other shops?' Jenny protested.

'We haven't finished shopping yet, darling.'

Kelly wondered about the dancing. What would it feel like to have Luc's arms round her, to be pressed to his body? Perhaps she ought to offer to leave early? But that would be ill-mannered. And she had to look after Jenny, didn't she?

Next, a strapless bra. More trouble buying underwear than Kelly had ever experienced before, but the fitter that

Madeleine had recommended was going to get the fit absolutely right.

Jenny was less interested in this, couldn't see the difference between one bra and another. But Kelly could feel the difference.

Finally, the jeweller's. It was so long since Kelly had bought or even thought about jewellery that she felt apprehensive entering the shop. What did she really want? Madeleine had given her a scrap of the fabric the dress was made of, and Kelly showed it to the elegant lady behind the counter. 'Have you any costume jewellery that might go with this? A pendant perhaps?'

Yes, the lady had something to match. Lots of things, in fact, and she was happy to display them all. Kelly and Jenny spent a blissful half-hour before picking a silver and amethyst pendant.

'Matching earrings?' the lady suggested. And that took another half-hour. Then Kelly felt she had to buy a small silver bangle for Jenny, who was overwhelmed.

Clutching their parcels, Kelly and Jenny went to the nearest café with a terrace and had a coffee and an orange juice. 'I'd quite forgotten just how much fun shopping could be,' Kelly said.

It was a great day for a wedding, sunny but not too hot. People would enjoy it. Kelly woke with a smile, she knew this was going to be a good day—for the bride and groom, for the wedding guests, for Jenny and Luc and herself.

Jenny was already awake and excited. The dress had been tried on the night before and was now waiting for her, hanging in a corner of the room. Madeleine had taken it in a little so the twirly bits weren't so obvious. But even though she had to stay in her wheelchair, Jenny was going to have a good time. Kelly's mood lifted even further when she saw the little girl's enthusiasm.

Jenny was washed and dressed and the two were considering what kind of wedding dress Jenny might have if, perhaps, one day, she got married. 'I do like bright red,' Jenny said.

'Not usual for a wedding dress,' Kelly suggested.

And then another voice. 'Since I have the day off I thought that we might all have breakfast together,' someone said.

It still happened, she could never get used to it. When first she heard Luc's voice, or saw him for the first time, there was that sudden increase in her heart beat, that thrill of excitement.

She had to hide it. But when she turned, saw how he was smiling at her, in perhaps that special way…the excitement only increased.

'Obviously Minette has the day off,' he went on. He had brought a large tray which held Jenny's usual cereal, yoghurt and fruit juice, and a continental breakfast for Kelly and himself. And somehow they managed to get the wheelchair and two seats round the little table.

'Now we're just like a real family,' Jenny said, 'all eating together.'

Kelly kept her head down, didn't dare look at Luc. She'd never really had a real family. She would have liked one.

But it was a good breakfast, and Jenny's chatter kept them all amused. When the meal was over Jenny turned to her bird book and Luc collected the dishes. He accepted Kelly's offer of help to carry them to the kitchen.

'A wedding,' he said. 'I suspect the first wedding you have been to since your own was planned. How do you feel?'

Kelly shrugged. 'It's a wedding and I'm looking forward to it. Nearly as much as Jenny is. I do remember planning my own but I'm well over it now, I realise I had a lucky escape. What about you? You planned a wedding and went through with it. What are your memories?'

He sighed. 'I was happy to get married but there didn't seem to be much joy in the occasion. And I certainly didn't plan the wedding. It was a carefully scripted event, it had to run exactly to plan. The photographers cost more than the choir and the clergyman—and I thought that was wrong.'

Kelly wondered whether to reach out to stroke his shoulder, but decided not to. This wasn't the time for gestures. 'I'm sure this wedding we're going to will be different,' she said. 'I'm really looking forward to it.' Then, she couldn't stop herself from asking. 'I know you've got jobs to do, but shall we see much of you?'

'Of course you'll see much of me! After the ceremonies I'll be sitting with you. I expect to dance with you.'

'Dance! I haven't danced in years!'

'Then it's time to start again.'

She'd be dancing with Luc. It was a dream of an idea.

It took Kelly over an hour to dress Jenny and then herself. But then they both agreed that they both looked very smart. And when Luc came for them—immaculate in a dark suit and dazzlingly white shirt and silver tie—it was obvious from his expression what he thought. 'You're so beautiful,' he whispered, adding quickly, 'Both of you.'

'We try,' said Kelly.

They set off for the wedding after the lightest of lunches. 'When Bretons feast, they do it in style,' Luc told her. They were driving to a village called Xavanne, about twelve kilometres away. By now Kelly was looking forward to the wedding as much as Jenny was. Dancing with Luc?

Xavanne was a typical small Breton village, with a church with a skeleton spire at one side of the square and the *mairie* at the other. The wedding seemed to be almost a communal affair—everyone Kelly saw appeared to be dressed up.

'This is a village wedding,' Luc told her, 'and the entire village wants to take part. Both bride and groom were born here. Jean, the groom, is a computer expert. Employed by the government, very much in the forefront of technology. But he wants the same kind of wedding as his parents and grandparents had. So does his bride. This will be the kind of wedding that could have happened a hundred and fifty years ago.'

He parked by the side of the village square, waved to a smiling girl aged about nineteen, who came hurrying towards them. 'This is Helene, another of Minette's grand-daughters,' he told Kelly. 'She'll stay with you, make sure you know where to go, what to do. And remember, you're among friends.' Then he hastened away.

'Kelly, what a lovely dress,' Helene said, with obvious awe in her voice, and Kelly decided that she liked her at once.

Kelly pushed the wheelchair down a side street lined with cheerfully shouting villagers. Then there was cheering and the sound of a band from further down the street, and Jenny asked in a panic, 'Where's my white ribbon?'

'I have it here,' Helene answered. 'Now, you hold

your end tight and cheer when my sister comes by.' She turned to Kelly and said, 'It is the custom before the wedding that the groom calls at the bride's home to claim her. Then the bride will walk to the church on the arm of her father. Guests follow and the groom comes at the end, holding the arm of his mother. And a band leads the procession.'

Kelly was fascinated.

The cheers and the sound of the band grew louder, and then the bride appeared. Helene took the end of Jenny's white ribbon and ran to the other side of the street, so that the tape formed a fragile barrier. The bride stepped up to the tape, held her bouquet in one hand, took out a pair of scissors, cut it and stepped past. The watchers cheered and the bride smiled. Then she walked on.

When she had passed Kelly saw that there were other children holding white ribbons to be cut. 'It is a symbol,' Helene said when she rejoined them. 'The couple must cut through difficulties. And did you see and smell the bouquet?'

'I did. The scent is lovely.'

'All the flowers, both bouquets and decorations, must be fragrant. The smell drives away evil spirits.'

'You seem to know a lot about wedding customs,' Kelly said.

Helene blushed, held out her hand to show a ring. 'Soon it will be my turn,' she said.

They followed the procession to the village square. First it was necessary to go to the *mairie*. Helene explained that the civil ceremony had to take place there—the church ceremony would come later. A small group entered the building, came out some minutes later and walked across the square to the church. 'But this is the proper wedding,' Helene whispered.

Kelly thought it was a lovely ceremony. The bride and groom sat under a carre—a large square of silk that prevented malice falling on them. They came out of the church through an arch of scented flowers and walked over laurel leaves. The spectators threw rice. All age-old customs—and Kelly loved them.

The reception was to be held in a large café in the square—and to cheers the newly married couple walked across to it. Jenny peered up at Kelly. 'How old do you have to be to get married?'

'You can't get married for a good few years yet,' Kelly told her.

'Do you have to have a house to get married?'

'Well, it's always a good idea.'

'Why aren't you married, Auntie Kelly? Would you like to be married and walk through the streets like this?'

The question made Kelly wince. 'I'd like to walk through the streets with all my friends and neighbours. And I haven't got married because I...I haven't met the right man yet.'

'You mustn't ask personal questions, Jenny,' a voice behind her said, and Kelly jumped.

'Luc! Where did you come from?'

'My duties are now over, I can enjoy myself with my family. Helene, it was good of you to look after Kelly and Jenny.'

'It was a pleasure. Kelly, when you do get married, have a French wedding.' And Helene left.

Enjoy myself with my family... Kelly thought of Luc's

words. If only… Someone had once told her that they were the two saddest words in the world.

'Did you enjoy the ceremony?' Luc asked her, and Kelly wrenched herself from dreaming.

'I thought it was wonderful. Everyone seems so happy!'

'Weddings should be full of joy—not occasions for formality. Now, let's go to find our places.'

He took her arm and led her across the square. Kelly knew that taking her arm was only a courteous gesture—but she did like it. She liked being so close to him.

He led her into a large café at the corner of the square. There were flowers everywhere, round the door, on the tables, decorating the pillars. And from somewhere the band had reappeared, were playing the sort of cheerful music that only an accordion band could play. They were greeted by the bride and groom and then found their table.

'You need to get your strength up for the dancing,' Luc told her, and she shivered, part fear, part anticipation.

Kelly thought it was the nicest wedding she had ever been to. The speeches were short, the cheering was loud. The bride and groom were told they had to drink out of a silver two-handled cup—the *coupe de mariage*—which had been in the bride's family for years. A bottle of champagne was placed on a bare table, a man dressed in an elaborate uniform drew out a sabre and with one carefully aimed slash cut off the neck of the bottle. The foaming liquid was poured into the silver cup.

'That man is dressed as one of Napoleon's hussars,' Luc whispered to her. 'Cutting off the neck of a bottle was one of their favourite tricks. If a woman truly loved and trusted the man, she would hold the bottle as he slashed.'

'I'll stick to a corkscrew,' Kelly whispered back.

Yes, it was a lovely wedding. There was food—but exactly what Kelly had difficulty in remembering afterwards. And then people just wandered around and talked to their friends. Luc didn't leave their table. Kelly realised it was because he didn't want her to feel abandoned—and she loved him for it.

Then the band struck up again. 'Just like in England,' Luc said, 'the bride and groom dance first—and then everyone joins in.' And it was as he said. The bride and groom danced first—to cheers—then others came to join them. 'Would you like to dance?' Luc asked.

She should have been expecting it, but the invitation came as a surprise and she was confused. She would love to dance with him but… 'I think I'd better stay here with Jenny,' she said.

'No! You've got to dance with Daddy. I want to see you dance!'

'Doesn't look as if you've got much choice,' Luc said with a grin.

He stood, held out his hand to her. She took the hand and he led her onto the floor. Feelings she couldn't describe flowed through her.

It was a simple, old-fashioned waltz. He put his arm round her waist, took her hand and swept her into the dance.

She loved it. She loved the music, the sense of rhythm, the feel of his arm round her, the gentle pressure of his hand. Occasionally, and necessarily, she had to lean against him and the feel of his body was so good. It was only dancing. She had to hold him and be held. But their bodies touched and it excited her. He said nothing but she could tell by the gleam in his eye that it excited him too.

They danced for another ten minutes and then he led her off the floor. Kelly knew it was necessary but she was sad. She could have danced for ever, she had been taken into another world. But now back to reality.

'Jenny must be getting tired,' Luc said. 'Perhaps we ought to be getting home. Is that all right with you?'

'Of course. I want Jenny to go away with happy memories of today. And I've had a lovely time but I'm getting a bit tired myself.' That wasn't entirely true. She wanted the magic of the day to continue—but she knew that the time was proper to leave.

Luc went to say a quick goodbye to the bride and groom and they left without too much fuss. The party was warming up—it was going to be a wedding to remember! But Jenny's eyes were closing. Time to go home.

Somehow they got back without Jenny falling completely asleep. Kelly suggested that she should put Jenny to bed while Luc changed. It only took her a moment to wriggle out of her wonderful new dress and into a thin sweater and trousers. Then a quick wash for Jenny—who was asleep in five minutes.

Luc came in then and tossed a parcel over to her. 'Your letters from Joe,' he said. 'It was on the hall table.' He bent over to kiss his sleeping daughter.

Kelly put the packet on a table. 'Doctor's mail.' She shrugged. 'Adverts for new drugs. I'll look at them in the morning.'

'It's still quite early,' he went on. 'The evening's only half-gone. Shall we open a bottle of wine?'

'I'd like that very much.' Half fearfully, she wondered what the rest of the evening might bring.

* * *

She appreciated his good red wine. She loved sitting with him, at ease on the couch, talking casually, like two old friends. She felt she had known him for ever—and it had only been four weeks.

'It was a good wedding,' he said, 'and I know they'll be happy. I would have liked a wedding like that myself—but we had to have a stuffy, formal, London wedding.'

Perhaps she had had just a little too much to drink, or perhaps she was tired. Her question was pointed but the same that he had asked a week ago. 'Would you get married again?'

She couldn't make out his expression. He looked alert but confused, as if he was making up his mind about something. She felt uneasy for a moment. 'Sorry, that was a bit personal, I didn't mean to—'

'I'll answer happily. Yes, I would like to get married again. Providing that I could find the right woman.'

The confused expression had gone. Whatever it was he had been thinking of, he had decided on an answer. He went on, 'But what about you, Kelly? Would you like to get married?'

This was dangerous ground. Carefully, she said, 'Yes, I think I would. But I'd have to be sure I was making the right decision.'

He said nothing for a while, as if considering her answer. So she went on, 'Marriage sounds wonderful, but at the moment I wonder if it's for me. Too much reliance on another person to make you happy can be dangerous. I feel safer being single. Luc, I'd be afraid to get married.'

'But you were going to marry Gary?'

'And look where love got me that time. I've learned better now. I'm happy on my own.'

'Completely on your own? You never talk about your family, Kelly. Are they supportive?'

She supposed it was a fair question. And she wanted to give him an honest answer. Too many times in the past she had avoided telling the truth. Taking a breath to settle her shaking nerves, she said, 'I have no family. I was an orphan, brought up by foster-parents. They were kind to me, I was well treated, but I learned from an early age to look after myself. To be self-sufficient. That was why the army was so good to me—and why I was good in the army. My one true friend, the family I never had, was Joe Cameron.'

'So you learned not to trust other people?' A quiet question.

'I'll give you a poetic answer. It's easier for me to trust people with my life than with my heart.'

He nodded, as if she had just confirmed something that he already knew. 'I'm not sure that I believe that entirely,' he said.

Then he shocked her by saying, 'You have a contract to stay here for three months. At the end of that time are you going to leave us? Never see me—or Jenny—again?'

It hurt so much when he said that. It was the last thing she wanted to do. But she knew that the alternative was dangerous. 'That would be very hard,' she managed to mumble.

Then she felt a crushing realisation and knew that she had to admit it to herself. It was a feeling that had been growing, she now knew she had been forcing herself to ignore it. But it was there.

She loved Luc.

She stood, tried to keep the expression in her face as

neutral as possible. 'It's getting late and we've both had a full day,' she said. 'I think I'll go to bed now.'

He stood too, they were face to face. She was staring at his wonderful, wonderful face and she knew exactly what he was thinking. 'I would miss you so much,' she said, and for some reason took a step nearer him.

He didn't speak, didn't move back. They were so close.

She didn't know why she did it, something other than her normal self made her do it. She leaned forward and kissed him. Just a gentle kiss but on his lips. He didn't move. His arms stayed by his sides, only their lips were touching. But it was so good.

And then… Flashback! Suddenly she wasn't standing in a French living room, kissing the man she loved. Suddenly she was a soldier again, in the desert. It was that last time. And they were under fire, the enemy was getting nearer. But even that wasn't as bad as the heat.

The obvious thing to do was to close the wound she was working on, send the patient back by helicopter, get out herself. She had been ordered to do that. But in the operating theatre—tent!—her word was law. She knew that if she closed the wound, sent him off, the patient would die.

Not if he had a chance here. Not if she was in charge.

She remembered the rush of adrenalin, it had supported her, she had carried on. I would do what *she wanted*! Not what was cautious. She had carried on, though it had been pointless.

Now she felt that same rush. She would do what *she wanted*! To hell with the consequences.

She wrapped her arms round Luc, pressed her body close to him. It was good, it was right. She felt his internal struggle as he wondered if this was right—and then his acceptance of what she was offering. He seized her, pulled her to him, kissed her with the same desperation that she felt.

His kiss was so good! Her doubts seemed to fall away, she was in ecstasy. But still in him she felt unease…why?

For a moment she pulled back from him—but not too far. Hoarsely she told him, 'I know what I'm doing. I'm my own woman now and I make my own decisions. You are not Dr Laforge now, you are Luc. You understand?'

There was tension in his voice as he replied. 'I know what I want, I want you. I've wanted you for weeks now, ever since we first met, and I know you want me too. But I still—'

'No buts! Luc, don't you want what I'm offering?'

There was no reply—not in words. Just a moan—and then a kiss that seemed to last for ever and yet promise so much more.

Eventually she broke away—but just for a moment. 'My bedroom,' she said, 'Tonight I need you in my bed.'

No more words. Just another kiss.

CHAPTER TEN

SHE led him by the hand to her bedroom. It seemed odd but still the right thing to do—they stopped on the way and went into Jenny's bedroom, both kissed the sleeping child on the forehead. Then they looked at each other. Something else that they shared.

So to her bedroom, and as Kelly pushed open the door she felt apprehensive again. She knew that this was what she wanted—needed even—but it was a step into a territory she had never explored before. Just how well did she know Luc?

She blinked. Had she left her bedroom like this? All she remembered was taking off her dress. Perhaps it was the fairies. Did they have fairies in France? Her bedroom looked…seductive. The shutters were closed, the curtains drawn, the room was in near darkness. There were two pools of dim light, from lamps on the dressing-table and the bedside cabinet. The covers had been partly turned back, the white sheets glowing against the rich red counterpane. Her nightdress was on the pillow. Why bother? She knew she was not going to need it.

Behind her, the door shut with a click. It was a good solid door, they would not disturb anyone.

Both stood silent for a moment and then he turned to take her in his arms. She looked up, his face was shadowed but she could see longing there and she knew she felt the same way.

His voice was low, 'Kelly, I still wonder…'

She put a finger to his lips, stopped him speaking. 'Are we going to have a debate or are we going to make love?' she teased. 'Luc, I know what I want and I want it as desperately as you do.'

It was all the reassurance that he needed. His mouth crashed down on hers and she knew, half fearfully, half happily, that now there was no going back.

At first he didn't seem to want to move. He stood there kissing her and she was happy for him to do so. She thought—it was hard to think at this moment—that she had reached a turning point, that her life would be totally different after this. And then she decided not to think. Now was a time just to feel.

He was kissing her. Then his arms relaxed their grip a little, she felt his hands slip under the hem of her sweater, ease it upwards. So she stepped back, lifted her arms over her head. She let him take the garment from her, throw it onto a chair. He groaned as he surveyed her body, half-revealed by the lacy white bra. And then she groaned too as he bent his head to kiss the swell of her breasts.

And now his hands were at her waist, undoing her belt so her trousers slipped downwards. She kicked off her shoes, so she could step out of them. Then she looked at Luc, proud of her womanhood.

He took her hands in his, moved backwards so he could

look at her. 'Kelly, you are so beautiful,' he murmured, 'so beautiful.'

She squeezed his hands. 'I'm still half-dressed. And you are entirely dressed.'

Another long kiss and then he undid her bra, threw that to one side too. There was something almost ritualistic in the way that he was undressing her, slow step by slow step. She realised that it was exciting her, making her need him more than ever. Making her love him more than ever! Now, there was a thought!

One last step. He knelt before her, placed his fingertips under the elastic and slid down her white lace knickers. Slowly slowly, his fingertips trailing along the sides of her legs, and she shivered with excitement. What was this man doing to her?

He was arousing emotions in her that had been dormant for years. He was making her feel like a full woman. Because he was a man and he wanted, needed, loved her.

Kelly kicked the scrap of white lace to one side. But he remained kneeling in front of her. His hands held her thighs, he bent his head forward and kissed her—there! The merest brush of his lips but that touch held a promise of so much more that she had to sob in anticipation. She felt that things were now moving with a speed, a logic of their own.

He stood, lifted her bodily, carried her to the bed. Such strength! And she was no slight slip of a girl. He laid her gently where the bed was turned back, stole a quick kiss. Then she watched through half-closed eyes as he dragged off his own clothes, threw them wherever they might land.

She smiled, lifted her arms behind her head, knowing what effect it would have on him. She looked at him again.

A well-muscled man, she knew that. And now his longing for her was obvious.

Then he lay by her side, an arm under her head. A soft kiss on the lips. 'This should go on and on,' he murmured. 'I want to take all night making love to you, there are so many things we can do together and all of them wonderful.'

Just one finger traced a line from her lips down to a thrusting nipple. He went on, 'But I don't think that I can hold myself back. I want you all now.'

'There will be time Luc,' she whispered back, 'there will be time… Oh, Luc!'

His head had bent to her breasts, he took each nipple in turn into his mouth and his tongue caused her such delight that she had to cry out. 'Luc, oh, Luc! Oh, that's so lovely, Luc!'

She could feel his urgency against her thigh, could feel the dampness below that told her that she was so, so ready. She bent her head to kiss him again, then stretched an arm round his waist, tried to pull him on top of her. He needed no further encouragement.

For a moment he was poised above her. She looked at those blue eyes, so full of excitement and longing and…love? Then slowly, so slowly, he entered her and her world dissolved in a whirlpool of pleasure. They were so good together!

She knew what he wanted, needed, it gave her so much pleasure to offer it to him. Perhaps it would have been better to take longer, to protract the pleasure until desire became un-endurable. But tonight that was not to be. Their bodies were as one and they moved together, their passion increasing until there was that explosion of sensation, until they jointly reached that pinnacle of pleasure and cried out their delight.

Gently he lay by her side. Their two bodies were damp with pleasure, both were breathing as if they had run a marathon. He reached out to caress a breast. 'You made me so happy,' he said. 'Kelly, I love you.'

What could she reply? 'Yes,' she said, 'and I love you.'

She was woken very early by birdsong. Luc was still asleep. She put on her dressing-gown and slipped out to the kitchen. When she returned she waved the aromatic coffee-pot under his nose and he woke at once. 'Breakfast in bed,' she said. 'Just coffee and croissants.'

He made a sleepy grab for her, which she evaded easily. Mournfully, he said, 'I'd rather have you.'

'Well, perhaps you can later. But first we'll have coffee. Move over.'

He moved over and they drank coffee. Then they made love to each other, slowly and languorously, again and again, till she felt that there could be no more joy in the world than what she had shared with him.

'I'm going to sleep again now,' she muttered. 'It'll be a couple more hours before Jenny wakes up. Perhaps you'd better go back to your own bed.'

'I don't want to leave you.'

'And I don't want you to go. But you know it's the right thing to do.'

'Perhaps so. Kelly, you know we have to talk. About us. About how we feel for each other.'

'Not now. What I have to do now is sleep, and that's all your fault.' She considered a moment. 'Well, perhaps a bit my fault.'

'Okay, I'll go. I'll take the coffee-tray with me.' He bent

over the bed, kissed her now closed eyes. 'Kelly, last night was the best night of my life. I love you.'

'Mmm,' she murmured. She was asleep.

She slept for an hour, then woke and was instantly alert. There was an hour before Jenny would wake, she had decisions to make. Last night had been magic—the most magic night ever. But now it was morning and she had to examine her life in the cool light of day.

Luc had said that he loved her, said it more than once. She believed him and, what was worse, she knew that she loved him back.

What would be the natural result of their love for each other? Time would tell but probably he'd ask her to marry him. Did she want to marry him? More than anything else in the world. Did she dare marry him? The more she thought about it, the more uncertain she became.

Then she smiled. It was Sunday. She had promised that today she would either sleep with him or leave him. Well, she seemed to have made that decision a day early. She had slept with him—so she couldn't leave. And, yes, it was her fault.

She dressed, went to see Jenny. Not in her room? Strange. Luc must have come to fetch her, wheeled her into the main house.

On Jenny's bedside table Kelly saw the packet of letters that Luc had brought for her the night before. She may as well take the packet to her bedroom, see if there was anything of interest.

The usual pile of advertising material that went straight into the bin. A brief, friendly note from Joe. A thicker, official-looking envelope with a foreign stamp.

She opened the thick letter. It was from New Zealand and offered her the job she had applied for—the one she had thought would be perfect for her. She'd almost forgotten the application form she'd filled in four weeks before, her life had been too busy. It had seemed a great opportunity then but now…she had other things to think of.

Dismayed, she put the letter to one side. What was she to do? Her life was different now, there was Luc and Jenny and… She shook her head. Too much to think about!

There was one other letter, quite large with something stiff inside. Still wondering about New Zealand, Kelly slit it open, glanced at the card. And dropped it as if it had been red hot. It was written in green ink!

She stared at it, then bent over to pick it up. It was a wedding invitation. She was invited to the wedding of Miss Evelyn Paget and Mr Gary Green. There was a pencilled note across the bottom. *Do come, Kelly. We can be friends and chat about old times.* Was the man mad?

Suddenly, Kelly's world was shaken. The things that had seemed to be certain to her were now uncertain. She remembered how much in love with Gary she had been. She even remembered the fun they had had selecting their wedding invitations. She also remembered burning them. Was she going to…? Did she think she was in love again? Could her love have the same result?

She ran to her bathroom, drank a glass of cold water and then sponged her face. She needed…she didn't know what she needed, perhaps reassurance of some kind. She needed to see Luc! But where was he?

She ran through Jenny's room, turned into the corridor. There were sounds of a cheerful conversation coming from ahead. Jenny's happy voice, the darker tones of Luc and something else. A woman's voice that Kelly didn't recognise.

She turned the corner, looked into the main hall. The front doors were open, outside she could see a sleek red sports car. In the middle of the hall was a party of three. Jenny, Luc and a smartly dressed woman who Kelly recognised at once as Luc's ex-wife. His ex-wife was kissing Luc. And it was not the polite, formal kiss on each cheek that the French gave so often. This seemed to be the kiss of a lover. And Jenny was looking on, delighted.

'I've missed this place so much,' Kelly heard Merryl trill. 'After London it's so, so wonderful. Luc, can we go for a walk outside? Take Jenny? I'd like to so much.'

'Whatever you want,' Luc said, smiling at her. 'In fact, let's go now and then—'

Kelly had not been seen yet. She turned, hoping to make her escape undetected, but Luc had seen her. 'Kelly! Come and meet Merryl.'

It was the last thing she wanted but now she had no choice. Merryl held out her hand. 'It's so good to meet you at last, Kelly. Jenny has been telling me all about you—but Luc has said hardly anything. Trying to keep you a secret!'

At first, her smile looked welcoming, sincere. But Kelly noticed the expensive clothes, the expertly applied make-up, the hair that had obviously been adjusted minutes before Merryl had entered the house. With Merryl, appearance was obviously everything.

Somehow Kelly managed to return the smile. 'Luc kindly offered me somewhere to live for a while because my own home was damaged. And I've enjoyed being here and spending time with Jenny.'

'This is a lovely house, isn't it? I was always so happy here.'

Kelly glanced at Luc. But for once his face was impassive. Whatever he was feeling, he would not let it show.

'Anyway, Kelly, Luc, Jenny and I are just going for a quick walk around the gardens. We need to chat about old times. Hope to see you later, after breakfast.'

'That will be nice,' Kelly managed to say. She had been dismissed. Just as if she were a servant. For a moment she had the urge to scream that last night she had slept with Luc, that it had been the most magic moment of her life, that he had said that he loved her. Once again she glanced at Luc. But his neutral expression showed her that she would get no help there.

'Perhaps see you after breakfast, then,' she muttered. Then she turned and walked away.

She sat on her bed and tried to think, coolly, dispassionately. She couldn't. Conflicting emotions warred within her so that she just didn't know what to feel or think.

Last night had been so wonderful. When she thought about it she knew that never again would she feel for anyone what she felt for Luc. She had thought she'd been in love with Gary, now she knew that she was capable of a far greater love. But Gary had caused her—was still causing her—so much pain and humiliation.

So the obvious next, terrible thought. How would she feel if she lost Luc? It would be unbearable. Better by far not to fall into the trap, to remain distant. She knew it would hurt very much to part from him now. She also knew that it would hurt infinitely more if she stayed with him much longer.

She thought of Gary, she thought of Merryl and slowly she came to a conclusion. She just dared not embark upon another love affair. She wasn't strong enough. And taking a job in New Zealand would make her decision absolute.

She hadn't brought much with her, it only took her ten minutes to pack. Then it was a case of stealing through the house, placing her bags in the car. Last of all, a letter to Luc.

Dear Luc,

We came to an agreement a week ago that today I would either sleep with you or leave you. I'm leaving you. And I'm so sad. Knowing you—and Jenny—has meant so much to me. But I still do not have the confidence to begin an affair that might bring me so much misery again.

I am sure we can continue to work together over the coming weeks. I will try to keep away from you as much as possible.

I hope you can take this as the last word between us and not try to get in touch. Since it is now largely repaired I am moving back into Joe Cameron's cottage.

Give my love to Jenny.

Kelly.

Kelly wiped away a tear, tiptoed out to her car and drove away.

Of course, Luc ignored her plea and came round to see her that evening.

'What rubbish is this?' he asked, waving her note at her.

Kelly wouldn't move from her doorway, wouldn't let him in. That would be fatal. 'I'm sorry, Luc, but this is the way it has to be. I just don't have the confidence. I saw you this morning with your ex-wife and—'

'Merryl has already headed back to England. Believe it or not, she had a photographer waiting for her outside the house. She thought she could persuade me to let her have pictures taken with Jenny. When she saw that there was no way she was going to have her own way, eventually she went.'

'You seemed pretty close to her.'

He shrugged. 'I needed to be polite. I learned early never to give Merryl any reason to start an argument. Especially when Jenny was around. And if I'd been cold to her there'd have been a screaming argument in the hall. As it was, I managed to get Minette to take Jenny for a walk before the screaming started.'

'I see,' said Kelly, and she did see. But now she had made up her mind. Being with Gary had taught her that once you took a major decision, you stuck to it. Less pain that way.

'Kelly, I'm missing you. Jenny's missing you. You're one of us.'

'And I'm missing you both too! I was happy with you both. I'm sorry, Luc, but I just daren't take the risk.' Now there were tears running down her face. But she never cried!

'Kelly, it might be hard for you to take a risk on falling in love again—but it's been hard for me too! I vowed never to look seriously at another woman. Then you came along and…well, I changed my mind. But it wasn't easy! I fell in love with you in spite of myself. And I thought we'd be happy together.'

'Perhaps you're stronger than me,' she said.

He was silent for a while. Kelly could tell he had something still to say, was trying to find the right words. And eventually, 'I love…or I loved you, Kelly. But if this is what you want, we will part. Just one thing. If we part now then we part forever. Which is it to be?'

For ever. What final words. But she knew it had to be. 'We have to part,' she said.

Now his face was as hard as iron. 'Very well. Working together after this would be impossible. I don't want you to come to the surgery again. I will see, however, that you are paid for the time you are contracted for.'

'There is no need. I am not short of money.' She shut the door.

Kelly thought that she was back where she had started. But Joe's cottage wasn't a refuge any more. She still went for her long walks, kept the cottage scrupulously tidy.

She missed her bedroom in Luc's home. She missed the life she had been leading, missed Jenny, above all she missed Luc.

She wondered what the future might bring her, she even wondered if she had a future. There was no need for her to accept the New Zealand job at once, she had six weeks to make up her mind. She didn't complete the acceptance, she supposed she'd go but she had no great interest in it.

Again and again she went over what she had done. Had it been the right decision to leave Luc? Yes! It had to be! Look at the state she was in now. And it could have turned into something far far worse.

Then suddenly, three days later, her life was turned upside down, a shock far greater than she had ever been able to imagine. It was a warm early evening, she was sitting outside on the cottage terrace, thinking blankly that everything around her was beautiful—and she just didn't care.

Her phone rang. She looked at it suspiciously, there was absolutely no one whom she wished to talk to. There were few people who would wish to talk to her. So she let it ring. But it rang and rang. Someone was determined to speak to her. It was less trouble to answer.

'Kelly, this is Paul Briard.' The voice was anxious. Hastily he said, 'Please don't ring off, this is very important. I need you urgently.'

'What is it, Paul?'

When he spoke she could hear the worry in his voice. 'This morning Luc went for a stroll in the woods near his home.' Now there was bitterness in his voice. 'There were hunters in the woods. It was probably an accident—but Luc was shot in the back. Not a shotgun wound either. He has a bullet in his spine. He needs urgent surgical attention. The hunters sent for SAMU—they're now being questioned by the police. SAMU brought Luc here.'

It was weird. She knew she should have been shocked, horrified by the news. But instead she reverted into the mindset she'd developed as a military doctor. Never mind that he was the man she loved most in the world. She had to be calm, passionless. 'How bad is the wound?'

'Serious. We've got him stabilised, he's even half-conscious.'

'Any paralysis?' Always a great fear when there was damage to the spine.

'Not yet. We've got him immobilised. But the X-rays aren't good. He needs urgent specialist care.'

'He needs a full neurological team to look at him. Can you get him to the hospital?'

'It's far too far away. My medical opinion is that he should not be moved if it is at all possible to deal with him here.'

'There! At the surgery? Have you found a surgeon?'

'There's one on holiday locally. I've sent for him. Kelly, we could do with your advice.'

'Of course. I'll drive there at once. Don't start anything serious until I get there.'

It struck her as she replaced the receiver that she was giving orders again. And expecting them to be obeyed.

Her car drew up outside the surgery, there seemed to be quite a lot of cars there. Then she realised that this was a normal working day, the rest of the unit would be functioning as normal. As normal as was possible. She hurried into Reception. Paul met her there. 'How is he?' she asked.

'Okay at present, but the situation isn't good. Something has to be done quickly. That bullet could move at any moment. Do you want to come and see him?'

Yes, she did. He was the man she loved. The thought of him in this state was so horrific that… But she was here as a surgeon! Calmly she said, 'I'd like to see him in a moment. Before I do I want to see the X-rays, your report of what has happened so far. Tell me about the injury.'

'The wound is to the dorsal vertebrae. He was shot with a small-calibre, standard velocity bullet at quite long range. There appears to be no fragmentation and the bullet hasn't transacted the spinal column. But it's lodged between two vertebrae and if it moves another couple of centimetres…'

'Paraplegia or even quadraplegia.' Paralysis of the

lower body or even all the body. Kelly shivered. Not a good prognosis.

'And is this surgeon here yet?'

'He is. Albert Delacroix. He is in my office right now.' Paul paused a moment and then said, 'Referring to some of my medical textbooks.'

'What kind of surgeon is he?'

'He is training to be one. He has performed a number of operations—but largely under supervision.'

'Does he want to perform this operation?'

Kelly saw that Paul was choosing his words carefully. 'He is certain that something needs to be done at once.'

'I'd like to look at the X-rays and talk to him. Is the theatre ready for use? Can you act as anaesthetist? Is there someone to be scrub nurse?'

'Everything is ready. All we need is a surgeon.'

'Good.'

For a moment she wondered why Paul was looking at her in that slightly baffled way. Then she realised. This was a Kelly he'd never met before. A curt, efficient, professional doctor, able to make half a dozen life-or-death decisions in the course of a day. And be confident about them. And that was what she was!

She liked Albert Delacroix. He was younger than her. He was keen, earnest, obviously a very hard worker. He had studied the X-rays, drawn little diagrams, consulted Luc's textbooks on anatomy.

He also spoke excellent English. But he had never taken a bullet out of a spine.

He pointed to one of the X-rays. 'You see, Dr Blackman, cutting down for access to the bullet here would be difficult but possible. What I am not sure about is how then to extract the bullet.'

'A nudge in the wrong direction and you've damaged the spinal cord,' she said laconically. 'But if the operation isn't performed there will soon be damage anyway. This isn't one of those cases when we can wait and see.'

'I agree. We need to operate at once. I gather that you are acquainted with the patient?'

'I am.'

'So do you feel happy about performing an operation on a friend? It will be a tremendous strain on you. I am willing to operate, to do what I can. But my honest medical opinion is that you would do a better job.'

Kelly glanced at Paul, who had been standing silently, listening to the conversation. 'I'd like to see the patient for a minute first,' she said. 'How is he, Dr Briard?'

'Sedated. But he will be able to recognise you.'

'I'd like to see him for a minute. Then I'd like to scrub up. You have scrubs ready?'

'We have everything ready.'

So far she knew she had done very well. All personal feelings had been repressed, she was a surgeon again. But when she bent over her lover, saw his face lined with pain, suddenly she reverted to the haunted woman she had once been. In England she'd never be asked to operate on a family member or a friend, it was ridiculous! She just couldn't do this!

'Luc?' She knew her voice was quavering. 'Luc, it's Kelly.'

Slowly, his eyes opened, and he tried to smile.

His voice was only a croak. 'Kelly. You can do it.' Then his eyes closed and he didn't speak again.

For a moment she remained hunched over the bed, tears falling unchecked. Then she stood.

'I will attempt to remove this bullet. Albert, you will assist me. Paul, you are to be the anaesthetist and I gather you have someone who has experience as a scrub nurse. Now we all prepare and I will operate in fifteen minutes.'

She was standing there, gowned, masked, a scalpel in her hand. In the background there was the familiar chuntering of the anaesthetic machine. Lights bright overhead, green-clad figures near her, waiting for her orders.

Time to start work.

Slowly, delicately, she cut her way into Luc's body. She was pleased to see that her old skills had not deserted her. Follow the channel of the bullet, enlarge it where necessary, mind the nerves, the blood vessels. And finally she could see the bullet. This was the hardest part. 'Forceps,' she said.

She had to hold the bullet, withdraw it, not let it move a millimetre to the side. And, inevitably, it didn't want to move. She kept up the pressure, pulled, knowing that eventually it would have to come. Or slip. It didn't want to move. She could feel the tension around the table now. Everyone knew that this was the crisis point. Then she felt the tiniest alteration in resistance. The bullet moved.

Slowly, she drew it out. There was a ting as she dropped it into a dish held out for her. There was a sigh of relief from everyone.

This was supposed to be a team effort. 'Would you like to start closing?' she asked Albert.

CHAPTER ELEVEN

SHE stayed in the surgery until the next morning, waking every two hours to check up on Luc's progress. It was good. In the morning the ambulance arrived and there was just time for a word with her semi-conscious patient before he was driven away. 'Go and see Jenny,' he said, 'and then tomorrow will you come and see me?'

'I will.' Then she watched as Luc was carefully transferred to the ambulance. She would have liked to have gone with him. But there was an experienced nurse in attendance so Kelly knew there was no reason to.

She watched as the ambulance drove out of the surgery gates. Her responsibility had ended. Then, and only then, the tears came.

Paul came to stand by her side. His arm slipped round her shoulders, and she turned to him and wept, her head buried on his chest. He felt big and comforting but not like Luc.

'Your work for now is finished. You can go home,' he said. 'But you must decide which home you wish to go to.'

'Which home?' She didn't understand.

'You can go to Joe's cottage. Or you can go back to Luc's house and stay with Minette and Jenny. I talked with

Luc while you were having a shower this morning. Madeleine is going to stay over there for a few days. You being with her would make things...happier.'

There didn't seem to be much difficulty in choosing. Previous decisions were...previous. 'I'd like to go home to Luc's house,' she said.

Paul smiled. 'That is good. And there is a surprise waiting for you.'

'What kind of a surprise?'

'I think you will find it a pleasant one. Now, I think there is little point in anyone going to see Luc today. The medical team there will want to assess him, will not want to be bothered with visitors and will probably keep him in Intensive Care overnight. They will let me know how he is progressing, I will forward all news straight to you. But tomorrow I think—'

'I'll go tomorrow morning.'

'Good. Now, since I am doing the work of three doctors, I must go.'

Kelly blinked. She had forgotten that this was a busy surgery, that there would be patients coming in, decisions to be made, the normal work to be done. 'Would you like me to come back here full time when I'm sure that Luc is all right?'

'Please,' said Paul. 'I want this surgery back to the happy way it was before.'

There was no way she could think on the drive home. It took all her attention just to stay on the road. But eventually she pulled up outside the front of Luc's house and there waiting for her were three figures. Minette, Madeleine and holding Madeleine's hand a small figure was standing. Standing!

The figure waved. 'Auntie Kelly, you're back! And I've missed you. Look, I can walk now—well, nearly.' And Jenny took four careful steps.

Kelly ran towards the little girl, gathered her in her arms and hugged her. 'You look marvellous, darling. And soon you'll be running.'

'I'm to do a lot of swimming. Will you help me swim?'

'Yes,' said Kelly unsteadily, 'I'll help you swim.' Things were moving too fast for her. How had she managed the past few days without seeing Jenny?

'You look terrible,' Madeleine said practically. 'Come inside before you fall over.'

Paul had phoned, saying that Kelly was on her way. Minette had breakfast arranged, they all sat in Jenny's room.

She had her breakfast. Then Madeleine said, 'I'm not a doctor but I'm going to prescribe to you. You need sleep. Twice your eyes have closed while you've been eating, and you've had to force them open. So…'

'But I want to know how—'

'If there's any news about Luc, I'll come and tell you. But for now, sleep.'

She knew it made sense. She went to her room, had the quickest of baths. Then to bed—there was no nightie. With the faintest of smiles she remembered that the last time she had woken up in that bed, she had not been wearing a nightie.

She climbed into bed and slept.

Driving to the hospital next morning she felt considerably better. She was awake, alert, she felt smart in her doctor-going-to-hospital suit and a moderate amount of make-up. What she couldn't decide was what she was going to say to Luc. The last time they had met—that was, before she'd operated on him—he had made things very clear to her. *If we part now then we part for ever.* For ever. Even then it had seemed a long time.

She knew his character now, he was a determined man. He didn't like people who couldn't make up their minds. And that certainly seemed to include her. Well, she would just have to see.

It took some time to negotiate her way to Luc's bedside. It was difficult to decide—was she family, friend or doctor? But eventually she was there sitting by his bedside, looking down at him. Those glorious blue eyes opened. 'Come to check on my progress, Doctor?' he asked.

She burst into tears. 'You could have been killed! What would I have done then?'

It was he who reached for her hand. 'Could have been killed? I could have been paralysed if it hadn't been for you.'

'It wasn't me that operated! I couldn't have done it, the way I feel about you, I couldn't have put a scalpel anywhere near you. It was some no-feeling operating machine that took over my body. It told the helpless, frightened me that this was just a job, that emotion had no part in it.'

'It did a good job. The surgeon who examined me yesterday wants to offer you a job. And it wasn't a no-feeling machine that operated. It was you. I can only imagine what you went through, thinking what I'd feel if I had to operate on you. But you knew you'd done a good job, didn't you?'

'Things are always doubtful. And at one stage I didn't think I'd dare start, never mind carry on.'

She shook her head. There was something she didn't really understand herself. 'But something happened to me as I operated on you. I knew it was a risk, but I knew it was your best chance. I had to do it, even though I knew I'd have to live with the consequences if you died. I took that risk. And now I feel that there isn't any risk I can't take. Luc, I've got brave!'

'You've always been brave!'

'But now I know it. I feel that everything in my life is going to go well from now on. I know I'm confident—but I don't know why I know. And I know what I want.'

'And that is?'

'I want a second chance. You told me that if we parted then we parted for ever. And that was terrible.'

'I have no memory of saying any such thing,' he said placidly. 'You must have imagined it.'

She was silent a moment. Then, 'Yes, I must have imagined it.' It simplified things.

'Is there anything else I can put you right on? You do remember what we said to each other when we got out of bed that morning?'

'I remember,' she agreed. 'More or less, I remember. We said that we loved each other. And now that we've got the practicalities out of the way, I'd like to kiss you. Just lie there and endure it.' Nothing like being frank, was there?

So she kissed him. She was bent uncomfortably over a hospital bed, there was that faint but pervasive hospital smell, she knew she must be careful not to disturb him. So it was a gentle kiss but it was a kiss like coming home. It comforted her and excited her, it wiped out the bad memories of the past and promised so much for the future, it was just… How much nearer could she get to heaven?

'I have wanted to kiss you since the first time I saw you

in that crashed van,' he said. 'I've kissed you properly four times since then, and each time I've not been able to sleep afterwards because of the joy it brought me. And now I can have that joy for ever.'

Kelly thought of the way she had been feeling the evening before—she had been considering whether to go to New Zealand. And now see how she felt! Life couldn't be better.

'Something I've got to tell you, Luc, something I've said before but I want to say again.'

He looked at her in mild surprise. 'That is?'

'I love you, Luc Laforge. And I love your daughter too.'

'Now, that is very satisfying. 'Because we love you back.'

What more was there to say?

MEDICAL™ 2-in-1

Coming next month

HOT-SHOT SURGEON, CINDERELLA BRIDE
by Alison Roberts

Dancing with gorgeous surgeon Tony at a ball makes nurse Kelly feel like a princess – but come morning, it's just a memory. Little does she realise that Tony is searching for his Cinderella…

THE PLAYBOY DOCTOR CLAIMS HIS BRIDE
by Janice Lynn

Kasey Carmichael is horrified when she meets her new colleague – rebel doctor Eric is the man she shared one passionate night with! Now Eric must prove he can be trusted with Kasey's heart.

A SUMMER WEDDING AT WILLOWMERE
by Abigail Gordon

GP David Trelawney is wary of relationships, but longs to help nurse Laurel blossom in the warmth of Willowmere. Before summer is out, this handsome doctor will make her his bride!

MIRACLE: TWIN BABIES
by Fiona Lowe

Devastated at the news of her infertility, relationships were *not* on GP Kirby's agenda. Until she meets hot-shot doc Nick Dennison – the attraction is electric! Then a miracle occurs: Kirby is pregnant – with twins!

On sale 7th August 2009

Available at WHSmith, Tesco, ASDA, Eason and all good bookshops.
For full Mills & Boon range including eBooks visit
www.millsandboon.co.uk

MEDICAL™

0709/03b

Single titles coming next month

A SPECIAL KIND OF FAMILY
by Marion Lennox

When Dr Erin Carmody crashes her car and is
rescued by GP Dom Spencer, the intense attraction
between them knocks her sideways! As Erin begins
to heal, she realises that she belongs with
this handsome single father and his boys. But will
Dom ever trust that their love is truly real…?

EMERGENCY: WIFE LOST AND FOUND
by Carol Marinelli

Every doctor dreads recognising someone in Casualty,
so when James Morrell has to treat his unconscious
ex-wife Lorna, he's shocked! As she recovers, James
realises he doesn't want Lorna as his patient – he
wants her as his wife, this time forever!

On sale 7th August 2009

Available at WHSmith, Tesco, ASDA, Eason and all good bookshops.
For full Mills & Boon range including eBooks visit
www.millsandboon.co.uk

A beautiful collection of classic stories from your favourite Mills & Boon® authors

With Love... Helen Bianchin
Bought Brides
This marriage was going
to happen...
Available 17th July 2009

With Love... Lynne Graham
Virgin Brides
A virgin for his pleasure!
Available 21st August 2009

With Love... Lucy Monroe
Royal Brides
Wed at his royal command!
Available 18th September 2009

With Love... Penny Jordan
Passionate Brides
Seduced...
Available 16th October 2009

Collect all four!

2 FREE

BOOKS AND A SURPRISE GIFT!

We would like to take this opportunity to thank you for reading this Mills & Boon® book by offering you the chance to take TWO more special selected titles from the Medical™ series absolutely FREE! We're also making this offer to introduce you to the benefits of the Mills & Boon Book Club™—

★ **FREE home delivery**
★ **FREE gifts and competitions**
★ **FREE monthly Newsletter**
★ **Exclusive Mills & Boon Book Club offers**
★ **Books available before they're in the shops**

Accepting these FREE books and gift places you under no obligation to buy, you may cancel at any time, even after receiving your free shipment. Simply complete your details below and return the entire page to the address below. You don't even need a stamp!

YES! Please send me 2 free Medical books and a surprise gift. I understand that unless you hear from me, I will receive 4 super new titles every month for just £2.99 each, postage and packing free. I am under no obligation to purchase any books and may cancel my subscription at any time. The free books and gift will be mine to keep in any case.

M9ZEI

Ms/Mrs/Miss/Mr ....Initials ....

BLOCK CAPITALS PLEASE

Surname ....

Address ....

....

....Postcode..........................

Send this whole page to:
UK: FREEPOST CN8I, Croydon, CR9 3WZ